I0543589

Tracks

Isaac Hobbs

Littleton

Hideaway Publishing Company

hideawaypublishing.com

To my friends.

Isaac Hobbs Littleton
TRACKS

Tracks spreading far and wide,
Trying to find a place to hide,
Buried beneath the wooded brush,
As if constructed with a paintbrush.

Each leading their own path,
With unstrung yet calming wrath.
One of two must be taken,
Reappearing as if unshaken.

You may leave them both for the taking,
But soon the Earth will start quaking,
Beneath your feet sat on the tracks,
You must not relax.

And as the distant whistle blows,
You probably would have froze,
For now, you must pick a path,
So which way will you go?

-Isaac Hobbs Littleton

Prologue

Before we begin I would like to get a few points out of the way:

First, this book is entirely fiction. However, the places in it are very real. In fact, these are the places where I spent most of my childhood summers. Needless to say, I didn't exactly visit these places in the time period where this book takes place, 1984. Also, when I say that the places in this book are real I don't mean individual shops or stores. I'm talking about the town and the lake where this story takes place—Kingston, Oklahoma, a very small town where almost everybody knows each other. It's very quaint and would probably remind anyone of the 1980's even today! The lake is called Lake Texoma and it is the border between Texas and Oklahoma. In fact, you can see Texas and Oklahoma from the lake at the same time! It's also quite a hot-spot for people during the summers.

The second thing is that the friendships in this book are loosely based around the friendships that I have with my friends. Of course, not everything is the same—like the names—but the personalities of my characters are mainly what my friendships are like. For example, sometimes we tease each other and pretend to be mean—I think that's with every friendship—but when it really counts and our friends are sad and need someone to talk to, we'll be there for each other at the end of the day.

The third thing is that these books—even though they're split up into three different short parts—are meant to be read as one whole story. It says that this book is 'Part 1—Spring'. There will soon follow a 'Part 2—Summer' and a 'Part 3—Fall' but that's just because I felt like I had so much information and stuff I wanted to write about that I had to split it into separate parts. Otherwise, it would've ended up being one of those huge bulky books that were always too intimidating to pick up off the shelf. Once all three books are out, though, I will combine them into one final novel.

The next thing I would like to mention is that over the course of writing this book I became overly-attached to these characters. I often found myself sitting at my computer, in tears, whenever something bad or sad happened to these kids. I would also laugh out loud whenever I came up with a joke or a smart remark for one of them to say. I hope you find yourself just as intrigued and attached to these characters as I did.

Now that all of that is out of the way I would like to tell you how I got my inspiration for this book. It's not one of those cliché stories where I had a dream or anything of the sort. Honestly, I got my inspiration from a place. The place I was inspired by was my family's lake house. It's not actually in Kingston but it's on the outskirts of it. There are woods right behind the house that the kids explore and there's the lake. The last thing I was inspired by was the train tracks (obviously). There are actually train tracks that run through the woods and over Lake Texoma. Again, that's where I got this idea, but let me tell you a story.

Late one night, when I was around seven or eight, I was lying down on the pull-out mattress from the couch. We actually still have the couch today and will continue to use it quite a bit, though it's getting kind of small for us.

My dad was lying next to me and everything else in the house was totally silent. You could hear the cicadas buzzing, the crickets chirping, and the slight rustle of leaves as the wind shook their tired limbs in the night sky.

"Hey, dad?" I asked, slowly turning my head to face my dad, the slight rustling of leaves whispering in the background.

"Yeah, All-star?" He slowly opened his eyes as he looked down at me. They were as blue as the ocean, just like mine.

"Why did we have to move?" Our family had just moved from Edmond, Oklahoma to Texas where I currently live. However, the place we were at now was just our lake house. We didn't live there, we just spent a lot of time there during the summer. "I miss Ian and Mason and Rylan and William."

My dad paused as silence filled the empty space in the room. "I miss them too, All-star," he paused. I could see tears starting to form in his eyes. "They're good friends, aren't they?"

"Yeah," I nodded as if it were obvious. "I miss them—a lot."

Dad nodded and he held up a finger, "Yeah, but do you hear that?" A slight rumble in the distance echoed through the woods and into our lake house.

"Yeah," I nodded as I listened. It was faint, but if I focused hard enough I could hear it.

"That's the train," he paused and smiled.

I nodded and felt like I was about to start tearing up as well.

"And on that train are separate carts. Carts full of whos-its and whats-its and all-its galore. You get what I mean?" dad asked. I didn't respond. "Each cart has its' own purpose. To carry something from one place to another. It could vary from each cart or they could all be carrying the same thing. But the thing I know for sure is that without each individual cart serving its' purpose the train couldn't continue. The train is the bigger thing that all carts work together to accomplish." I was confused. "And in a lot of ways the carts on those trains are like people."

I raised an eyebrow, somewhat skeptical. "How so?"

"Well, people will come and go out of our lives—just like carts on trains come and go from one place to another. But if there's anything I'm sure of it's that the memory of that person will stay with us forever—and that's the foundation of those friendships; those are the **TRACKS**."

TRACKS

TRACKS

Part 1

Spring

May 11, 1984

Chapter 1

Secret Wars

Clink; clank; click—

Liam's bicycle chain popped in and out of place as he zoomed down the street and towards school. Liam had a blue backpack strapped tightly around his arms and waist so it wouldn't fall off of him when he was riding his bicycle. As the wheels spun, they made a whistling sound as air blew through the patterns of chains that held his tire in place.

His dirty blonde hair—sometimes mistaken for light brown—was blowing into his eyes as he continued to speed down his street. His blue eyes glistened in the faint, pink, rising sun on the horizon as he whizzed around the corner of his street. He turned the corner so fast that most people—traveling at that speed and around that sharp of a corner—would've tumbled off of their bicycle and slid across the road, covering them in bruises and gashes, but not Liam. Liam had pulled this stunt so many times that it was second nature. His back tire would screech and leave a black trail of burnt rubber behind him as Liam would shift his weight to the left and pop his front tire up preventing him from being one of the many people that would arrive at school with bruises and gashes. As Liam regained his balance he continued to pedal his way out of the neighborhood. The fact that he lived so close to the entrance and exit of his neighborhood made it easier for him to get to school and the comic shop than it did for his friends Jack and Johnny—who also lived in the same neighborhood.

Even though they all went to the same middle school and were all in 8th grade together, they hardly ever met up on the way to school. However, they would always meet up on the weekends and at school. Part of the reason was because Liam always left a little early so he could say "hi" to the homeless guy, Gabe, who lived right outside of Liam's favorite comic shop. Of course, the comic shop wasn't ever open that early—Liam just wanted to start off his day right by being nice to and encouraging Gabe.

The middle school was only a few minutes away from Liam's house, and the comic store was only one minute away and it was on the way to his school—so there was no harm done by saying "hi" to Gabe.

As Liam pulled up to the comic shop he slowed down and, as always, Gabe was sitting right outside holding a cardboard sign that said *'Please spare some change.'* The comic shop had an electronic sign that was usually lit up a bright red that said *'Comic Shop,'* but was turned off because it was too early. Liam didn't know the exact reason why Gabe was homeless, but he had to expect it had something to do with drugs—Gabe might have hinted at it a couple of times.

As Liam slowed down passing the comic shop he yelled, "Hey, Gabe!" And he started to wave.

Gabe seemed to have just woken up as he looked up at Liam and a huge friendly, toothless smile spread across his face. "Good morning, Liam!" And he started to wave.

"How you doin'?" Liam asked.

"Oh, the usual," Gabe smiled.

"Well, just wanted to check up on you and see how you were doing," Liam said as he slowly started to pick up pace, "See you later, Gabe!"

Gabe gave him a thumbs up, "Don't go an' get yourself into trouble now," Gabe hollered as Liam continued to drift away from the comic store and Gabe.

"I won't!" Liam yelled back as he continued to pick up pace towards his school.

Gabe chuckled as he shook his head happily and muttered to himself, "Nice lad," referring to Liam, as he continued to sit in front of the comic shop and hold his cardboard sign.

Gabe's two front teeth were missing and he was blind in one of his eyes. Gabe also had long brown hair but kept it in a hair tie that Liam had stolen from his mom and given to Gabe. Liam had also given Gabe an old hat that his dad wanted to throw away for last Christmas. It hid his man-bun perfectly. Gabe hadn't always sat in front of the comic shop—he had actually only recently started to stay there—but he decided that it was the best spot for him for now. He knew people; people were kind to him; he got to say good morning and, best of all, people leaving the comic shop would give him change. Well, most people at least. Gabe's face was covered in scars and his clothes were old and ragged. However, the clothes he had on now weren't nearly as bad as the ones he used to own. Liam had also given Gabe his dad's pair of old shoes when he got new ones. Gabe seemed really grateful for that. Although nobody knew how old Gabe was or whether he had a family or not, they knew that he was old enough to be a grandpa—he sure looked it at least. Nobody had really wanted to ask Gabe how old he was—it would probably come across rude to some adults—but knowing Gabe, he would've been perfectly fine with answering that question.

Liam slowed his bike down as he approached the front entrance of his middle school. He quickly hopped off of his moving bike and parked it into one of the front bike rack slots. After he parked his bike he walked inside of his school. As he walked inside a few kids were already there, but it was mainly empty. Liam walked up to his locker and began to open it up.

As he opened his locker he started to pull books and notebooks out of his backpack and put them into his locker. As he continued to do so he could see his friends pull up to the school out of the corner of his eye. They parked their bikes in the bike racks as they started to walk up to the school.

Liam's friends walked up to the school as the school bus pulled up and started to let kids out behind them. Kids started to swarm the hallways of the school while Liam's friends walked in.

"Are you excited?" Jack yelled, obviously excited as he walked up to Liam who was still pulling and putting books in and out of his locker and backpack. Jack was Asian, and he was the youngest member of their group at age thirteen. He wore a pair of big glasses that covered nearly his whole face, and he was only about five feet tall. He had straight, black hair that was combed over to the right and had an excessive amount of gel in it to keep it in place. He almost always wore a striped shirt and jeans, and constantly had a pencil tucked tidily on top of his ear. He also always wore black, shiny dress shoes with black dress socks underneath. He also had a red backpack strapped tightly around his arms.

"For what?" Liam chuckled as he continued to put books into his locker. Liam didn't know what Jack was referring to and was somewhat confused.

"For the *Secret Wars* comic!" Johnny yelled, even more excited than Jack. Johnny was white, like Liam, and he was the oldest one in the group. He was still the same age as Liam, fourteen, but older by just a couple months. Johnny continued, "Oh my God, I'm so excited!" He said as he pulled out an inhaler from his pocket and held it up to his mouth and breathed it in.

"I know, right! I've been waiting for this comic for so long," Liam continued as Johnny stuck his inhaler back into his pocket—his breathing calming down. Liam continued, "It was supposed to come out yesterday, but the comic shop didn't have it in stock yet!"

"Yeah!" Johnny continued, "Me and Jack—"

"Jack and I," Jack corrected as he pointed at Johnny with the back end of his eraser.

"Nobody cares, dude," Johnny continued, "My point is *Jack and I* are going to go to the comic shop after school to get it. Wanna come?"

"Well, duh," Liam continued, "I was already planning on going. Hey, and plus, look what I got," Liam said as he dug his right hand into his left pocket.

He reached down until his fingertips grabbed hold of the plastic bag in his pocket and yanked it out. The coins inside of the plastic bag bounced off of one another as they created a *jingling* sound. Liam continued, "Money!" There weren't any dollar bills in the bag, just quarters. "I was thinking, if we wanted to, that after going to the comic shop we could meet up at the arcade?"

Johnny looked over at Jack and shook his head as he returned his focus to Liam who had asked the question, "No, sorry dude. I went yesterday and I've wasted enough money for one week."

"Same—sorry Liam," Jack said, tucking his pencil back behind his right ear as he started to walk towards his locker.

"Oh, okay—it's fine," Liam said, obviously disappointed, but he didn't let Jack or Johnny know. He didn't want to guilt-trip them into going to the arcade anyway. "Well, I'll see you guys later," Liam said as he closed his locker. Jack and Johnny walked away to their lockers in separate directions.

As Liam held all of his books for his first period class under his right arm, a few lockers away from him a girl slammed her locker shut. She, too, had several books under her right arm and was walking away. She had brown, curly hair, and was about Liam's size and she wore a black hoodie with long sweatpants.

Most of the people that were in that hallway were already gone and walking to class, which left Liam and this girl in the same hallway alone. They both had first period together—and maybe a few other classes together—but Liam didn't notice it too much. What he really noticed was how she was at the comic shop almost as much as them. Every time that he, Jack, and Johnny were at the comic shop she would be reading or looking for comics just like them. Of course, Liam had remained too shy to actually go introduce himself to her, but it was pretty obvious—to his friends—that he liked her.

Liam pursed his lips as he walked to first period.

As Liam sat down at his desk the bell rang.

"Okay!" Mr. White, a dark-skinned African American, clapped his hands as he walked into class. "Who's ready to start the day off right?" His voice was always excited and energetic, which made this history class fun, unlike many other past history classes that Liam had had.

Almost immediately a hand shot up in the back. Liam didn't know this kid's name but he definitely recognized his face. He was that kid that constantly had to interrupt the teacher's lesson to make himself seem funny—in some cases making him look obnoxious which Liam thought was the funniest of all.

"Yes, uhm, Douglas," Mr. White scratched his mini-afro, knowing he was in for a treat.

The kid in the back, Douglas, put down his hand and asked, "How come kids get tardy if they don't get here on time, before the bell, but teachers like you can just walk into the classroom whenever you want?"

Mr. White pursed his lips and tapped his left temple as if saying *'I'm thinking.'* "You know what, Douglas—that is a very good point. I will definitely put that as one of my *top* priorities to figure out."

A couple of scattered kids around the room started to chuckle at Douglas and how Mr. White was being sarcastic, including Liam.

"Is that the only question there is?" Mr. White asked, nobody raising their hand, "Douglas—do you have another *important* question?"

Douglas shook his head in shame and embarrassment as a couple other kids began to start chuckling. As everyone chuckled Liam looked up to the front right of him where Carol sat. Carol was the girl that goes to the comic shop and who has a locker close to Liam. Liam sat in the middle of the room, and Carol sat one seat to the right and up of him. She too was laughing, and as she continued to laugh she turned her head and made eye contact with Liam. As she made eye contact with Liam, he immediately looked the opposite direction, trying to avoid her gaze. She too looked the opposite way. They both stopped laughing.

"Oh my God, oh my God," Liam muttered to himself as he buried his face in the palms of his hands. She saw him looking at her. She *saw* him. She probably thought that Liam was weird and creepy for looking at her. "Oh my God, oh my God—this sucks."

"Is there anything you'd like to share with the class, Liam?" Mr. White asked as the class grew quiet, "I thought I heard you say something."

"Nothing! It's nothing," Liam replied quickly, almost *too* quickly.

The class sat silent for what felt like forever until Mr. White spoke up again, "So, as I was saying," he clapped his hands again. It was a frequent thing he did to catch the students' attention, "Let's not end off this week badly—let's end it off fantastically! And, I know what some of you are probably thinking—*'Oh, history class is so boring; I wish I didn't have to take it'*—blah, blah, blah. Well, today, do I have a surprise for you!" Mr. White pulled out a huge map of the school from behind his desk, "We're gonna play a game!"

Liam quickly opened up his locker as he got ready for second period: science. As Liam fumbled over his notebooks Jack and Johnny walked over to him.

"Hey, you ready for science?" Jack asked. They all three had the same science class together and their science teacher had promised them a fun experiment that day.

Liam just nodded, "Yeah, sure." He didn't sound nearly as enthusiastic as Jack had.

Johnny and Jack shot each other a quick glance.

"Hey, you okay, Liam?" Johnny asked, "Or are you just upset because Carol's out of your league?" To be fair Johnny had no idea what had happened in history with Liam and Carol—he just liked to constantly tease Liam about it.

"Come on, man!" Jack slapped Johnny's chest with the back of his hand, "You can't just single her out—everyone's out of his league."

Johnny laughed, "Well, at least he doesn't have a stupid crush on Samantha—who, by the way, is out of all of our leagues, combined!"

Jack pursed his lips as he held a finger up to them, "Come on, man! Not so loudly!"

"What?" asked Johnny shrugging, "You don't want me to tell everyone that YOU HAVE A GIGANTIC CRUSH ON SAMANTHA BEASLEY?" He yelled this time causing almost everyone around them to turn and stare.

"Shut up, man! I'm serious!" Jack pursed his lips even tighter, "She's gonna hear you."

"Dude, she's not even around here—and why should you even worry about her knowing? If I were you I would worry about Ricky finding out," Johnny stated. Ricky was one of the most athletic kids in school and he was dating Samantha. They were pretty much put into the popular crowd the minute they started to date.

"I know—but word gets 'round," Jack said, "And I don't want people to go spreading my huge crush on Samantha around the school," Jack stated.

"SO, YOU ADMIT IT, JACK SIMONS?" yelled Johnny one last time as Jack turned around and started to walk away, shaking his head as his face turned bright red with embarrassment. He was done putting up with this.

As Jack walked away Johnny yelled, "I'M SORRY FOR TELLING EVERYONE THAT YOU HAVE A CRUSH ON SAMANTHA BEASLEY, JACK SIMONS! IF YOU TOLD ME YOU DIDN'T WANT PEOPLE TO KNOW ABOUT IT I WOULDN'T HAVE YELLED IT ACROSS THE WHOLE SCHOOL!"

Jack continued to walk away, his back facing Johnny as he ignored him. Johnny laughed as he pulled out his inhaler and held it up to his mouth.

Liam slammed his locker shut behind Johnny as he started to walk the same direction Jack had. Liam looked upset as well, but Johnny couldn't tell if it was with him or he was just in a bad mood.

"Oh, for crying out loud," Johnny muttered to himself, "GUYS, IT WAS A JOKE! COME ON!" he yelled as he ran after Jack and Johnny on their way to science class.

As they all walked into science class Johnny said, "Guys, I'm sorry."

"Don't worry about it, man," Jack said, "Just don't be a dope again."

Johnny chuckled, "No promises."

Jack smirked as they sat down at their desks. They sat in a straight row at the very front of the class. Mr. Phisel allowed them to choose where they sat at the beginning of the year and they haven't changed seats yet.

Once everyone was in the classroom and at their desks, Mr. Phisel walked into the classroom and sat down at his desk waiting for the bell to ring. Once it did, Mr. Phisel stood up and looked at the whole class, "Well, since it's Friday some students asked me if we could do something special today. The answer to that is yes!"

Jack, Johnny, and Liam started to exchange excited looks.

"I know, I know—it's not the end of the year yet, and we're all waiting for summer break, but we just need to push through for one more month! So, to make it easier for you guys not to fall asleep in my class, Andy, I have an experiment that I'm gonna need help with." Andy was notorious for falling asleep in class. He already had more detentions than anyone in the whole school just for falling asleep.

Everyone immediately raised their hand hoping that Mr. Phisel would pick them to help with this exciting experiment.

"I'm sorry for those of you who would like to help with the experiment, but I'm gonna have to let the gentlemen who gave me the idea to do something interesting today—So Jack, Johnny, Liam—would you guys join me upfront?" Mr. Phisel pointed at them as they stood up. They had told Mr. Phisel to do a fun experiment, but they didn't know what the experiment was or that they would get to participate.

As Jack, Johnny, and Liam walked up to the front of the classroom they gave each other surprised looks.

"So—here's what we're going to do," Mr. Phisel continued, "It's not a crazy experiment but we're going to be testing the weight of—" Mr. Phisel grabbed a balloon and sucked in as much helium as he could, *"The weight of certain gases!"* The helium had caused his voice to go super high pitched as the class started to laugh. "So," his voice was back to normal, "I bet you guys already knew about helium and how it makes your voice go really high."

Everyone in the class nodded along with Jack, Johnny, and Liam who had smiles stretched across their faces as they waited excitedly to see what they would get to do.

"But did you guys know about sulfur hexafluoride?" asked Mr. Phisel.

Everybody shook their heads.

"Well, helium is six times lighter than air—so can anyone guess what sulfur hexafluoride is?"

Jack raised his hand even though he was standing right next to Mr. Phisel.

"Yes, Jack?" asked Mr. Phisel.

"Is it six times heavier than air?" asked Jack.

Mr. Phisel's eyes lit up, "Yes! In fact, whenever you breathe in helium—six times lighter than air— your voice gets higher, but whenever you breathe sulfur hexafluoride—six times heavier than air—your voice gets lower!"

"Nice," Johnny muttered to himself, a huge smile stretching across his face.

"Would you guys like to try?" asked Mr. Phisel holding out the balloon full of sulfur hexafluoride—a blue one. The one full of helium was red.

Jack, Johnny, and Liam nodded excitedly.

"Okay—but I have to warn you, don't inhale too much because it could be unhealthy, okay?"

They all nodded in agreement.

"Oh, and also, one more thing," Mr. Phisel said, "I have a question for you guys, and if you guys don't get it right then someone else might just get a chance to do this instead of you."

The whole class hushed as murmurs started to erupt.

"Why is helium in the red balloon, and why is sulfur hexafluoride in the blue balloon?" Mr. Phisel questioned, "You should know this."

"I know!" Jack yelled, his hand shooting up into the air.

"Yes Jack?"

"Helium is in the red balloon because it causes your voice to sound higher, and red stands for hot or warm, and hot or warm water and air rises, like our voices when we inhale that—also the sulfur hexafluoride is in the blue because blue stands for cold or cool, and cold or cool air or water sinks or lowers like our voice when we inhale that gas!"

Mr. Phisel smiled, "Okay, not exactly what I was looking for but I'll take it. That's very impressive by how fast you could connect the dots like that though."

"Thank you."

Mr. Phisel held out both of the balloons—the red and the blue—the helium and the sulfur hexafluoride. "Choose whichever one you'd like—but only one." He raised an eyebrow as he looked at Jack, as he thought about which one to pick. Finally, Jack picked the red one with helium in it and held it tight. "Don't inhale that just yet," Mr. Phisel said, "Let's wait until I explain what to do."

"Okay," Jack nodded.

"Now which one of you wants to do the sulfur hexafluoride?" asked Mr. Phisel walking up to Liam and Johnny.

"He can do it," Liam said pointing at Johnny.

Johnny's eyes lit up with excitement, "Really dude?" he asked gratefully.

"Yeah, go ahead."

"Thanks, dude."

"Well, okay, I guess," Mr. Phisel said handing the blue balloon to Johnny as Liam went and sat back down at his seat. He didn't care too much about the gas inside of the balloon—he just thought it would be funny to hear his friends talk with a funny voice.

"Okay," Mr. Phisel continued, "Here's how this is gonna work. They're both gonna say somethin' funny, and whoever we laugh at the most wins."

Johnny smiled; he basically already won.

"So, what you wanna do is blow all of the air out of your lungs and then suck what's inside the balloon, okay?" Mr. Phisel clarified.

Jack and Johnny both nodded.

"Jack, you'll go first, and Johnny, you'll go second. You'll go back and forth until all the gas in the balloon is gone and then our winner will be voted for," Mr. Phisel said.

There wasn't much gas in each balloon—just enough to get a few laughs in before they ran out.

"Ready—set—go!" Mr. Phisel yelled as Jack blew out all of his air and breathed in helium.

"I sure do hope I hit puberty soon," Jack said.

"At least you don't sound like Darth friggin' Vader!" Johnny replied.

The rest of the conversation was really inaudible and nobody could really understand what they said, but everyone was still laughing hysterically.

After about three minutes of inaudible talking, Mr. Phisel intervened, "Okay, we're gonna have to end it off there."

"Oh, come on, I was just gettin' started," Johnny said in his deep sulfur hexafluoride voice.

The whole class laughed.

"So, we're gonna have a vote. Raise your hand if you think Jack should win," Mr. Phisel said.

About six people out of twenty raised their hands.

"And Johnny," Mr. Phisel pointed at Johnny

Everybody else raised their hands.

"Well, it's settled then—Johnny is the winner! Your prize is—" Mr. Phisel threw a piece of candy at

Johnny. Johnny tried to catch it but dropped it as it fell on the ground.

"Crap," his voice was still very low, and was taking a while to wear off. The whole class laughed again.

"Jack," Mr. Phisel, "Nice try, buddy. Maybe next time."

Jack pursed his lips and snapped as if saying *'Dang it,'* as he walked back to his seat to the left of Liam.

"So, what have we learned today?" asked Mr. Phisel.

"That it's a lot easier to be funny when your voice is screwed up," Johnny said walking back to his seat, a sucker in his mouth that Mr. Phisel gave to him.

"Well," Mr. Phisel chuckled, "Besides that."

Nobody answered.

"Okay, to be honest neither do I. I was just hoping that one of you guys would say something and then I could agree with you," Mr. Phisel laughed, "Guess it was just for fun."

The bell rung.

"Well, see you guys later, that's the bell," Mr. Phisel said as he waved the students off.

"You're the best, Frizzle," Johnny said, "See you around."

"Bye Johnny," Mr. Phisel replied, "See you guys later!"

Later that day, Jack, Johnny, and Liam sat at the lunch table together and started to eat lunch.

"Did you bring it?" asked Johnny looking at Jack.

Jack smiled and nodded as he pulled out a brownie from his lunchbox. Jack handed Johnny the brownie and Johnny handed Jack a soda—Dr. Pepper to be more precise.

You see, Johnny wasn't allowed to have chocolate and Jack wasn't allowed to have caffeine so it was a win-win.

Across the whole cafeteria Ricky Jason sat with some of the athletic kids. To be fair it wasn't just the athletic kids and not *all* of the athletic kids sat there. Only about four kids actually sat there that were on the football team, and most of the others were just Ricky's friends.

"Dude, I'm sorry," Ricky said to his friends, "I can't make the party. I have a lot of family stuff going on." Ricky was a dark-skinned African American and had a short buzz-cut with specific designs on the side of his head in his hair. Plus, he was always wearing his sport sweater.

"Sounds to me like he just wants to hang out with Samantha all day long," one of Ricky's friends, Will Tucker, said.

A few other people nodded. They had a party this weekend and Ricky couldn't go due to family business, but all of his friends were convinced that it was because he had plans with Samantha.

"Okay—how can I make it up to you guys?" Ricky asked.

Will tapped his head as he thought, "Oh! I have an idea," he continued, "How about you go sit with weasel, nerd, and loser," he pointed to Johnny, Jack, and Liam.

"Come on, guys," Ricky said.

31

"Go sit with them, now, and then we'll see how much you wanna come hang out with us," Will said.

Ricky pursed his lips as he stood up and mouthed the word *'fine.'*

They called Johnny weasel because whenever he didn't have his proper asthma medication he would wheeze and have trouble breathing. Hence the name weasel.

They called Jack nerd—well that one should be pretty self-explanatory.

And they called Liam a loser because he hung out with Jack and Johnny.

As Ricky walked over to Johnny, Liam, and Jack the rest of Ricky's friends started to laugh hysterically. Ricky sat down right next to Liam and right as he did Liam, Jack, and Johnny stopped talking and just looked at him.

They stayed silent for about thirty seconds until Johnny spoke up, "Is this some kinda joke?"

Ricky squinted, "I'm not sure I know what you mean," He knew it was a joke but he could at least have a little fun with these guys before he left.

"What are you doing here?" asked Jack curiously. He too was skeptical.

"Just thought I'd come sit with you guys today," Ricky said.

Everyone remained silent again until Johnny spoke up again, "Can you please leave. Not to sound mean or anything, but we don't really like to hang out with you and people in your friend group. They tend to be jerks."

Ricky did his best impression of someone who was offended, and he did a pretty good job as he said,

"God. Just wanted to find someone to eat lunch with," as he stood up and started to walk away.

Liam looked at Johnny and pursed his lips, "Wait," he said. Ricky stopped and turned around to face Liam, "You can sit here if you want."

"Bro—what the heck?" asked Johnny.

"Thanks, dude," Ricky said as he sat down again, "And I do understand why you would be kinda skeptical," Ricky said to Johnny.

Johnny nodded, still skeptical.

"Well, I'm Liam."

"Johnny."

"Jack."

"Well," Ricky continued, "Nice to meet you."

Liam nodded as an awkward silence filled the air.

"What're you guys doing this weekend?" Ricky asked, "Maybe we could hang out."

Johnny pursed his lips and shook his head as if it were obvious what Ricky was doing.

"Yeah, we're going to the comic shop after school if you'd like to meet us there," Liam said.

"Dude, stop," Johnny said, "It's a trap."

Liam shook his head, "Dude, it's not a friggin' trap."

"Whatever," Johnny said before leaning over to Jack who sat next to him and whispered, "It's a trap."

Jack simply nodded as Liam and Ricky continued to talk.

"Totally," Ricky said, "I'll be there."

"Okay," Liam said, "Well, see you later."

Ricky nodded as he stood up and walked over to the table where Will and the rest of their friend group sat. Once Ricky sat back down they all started to laugh.

"Hey, they're going to the comic shop after school," Ricky said, "We could *meet* them there if we wanted to."

Will reached out his hand across the table in a fist, "Nice."

Ricky gave him a fist-bump. "Guess we'll see them at the comic shop."

As Ricky and his friends laughed, Liam, Jack, and Johnny sat at their table.

"Okay," Liam said looking over at Ricky laughing with all of the other kids, "It's definitely a trap."

"Yeah, no dip—that's what I said!" Johnny said angrily.

"So, what? Are we just not going to go to the comic shop after school?" Jack questioned.

"No," Liam continued, "Of course we're gonna go—we'll just have to get there first—in and out."

Johnny nodded, "Sounds like a plan—on the other hand we could stay and let Jack and Ricky fight it out for Samantha."

"Yeah right," Jack laughed, "Wait—HEY!"

Johnny laughed as the bell rang once again, dismissing them from lunch.

The last bell of the day rang, dismissing all of the students for the weekend.

It was peaceful and quiet outside as the gentle breeze of the hot afternoon rustled the green leaves on the trees and swayed the green grass back and forth.

The sun was overhead as the birds chirped in the silent afternoon wind.

Jack, Johnny, and Liam busted out of the front doors and were the first people outside as they hopped on their bikes and zoomed off down the street toward the comic shop.

They pedaled as fast as their legs could carry them as they raced off of the schoolyard.

They didn't slow on any of the curves or turns and when they approached the comic store they jumped off of their bicycles allowing them to crash against the comic shop outside walls next to Gabe, the homeless guy.

"Hello, boys," Gabe said as they hopped off their bicycles.

Nobody responded. They were all in too much of a hurry to hear him.

Gabe didn't say anymore, he just nodded as everyone ran inside the shop. Behind the counter was Glenn. He greeted the familiar faces of Jack, Johnny and Liam.

"Hey, guys! Ready for the weekend?" he asked them.

"Not now, Glenn," Johnny said.

"Sorry, we're in a hurry," Liam and Jack said at the same time.

"Secret Wars?" asked Glenn.

"Yes!" Liam said pulling out his bag of money and practically throwing the quarters at Glenn.

"You know," Glenn said as he counted the quarters, "This comic was supposed to come out yesterday on May 10, but we didn't receive our package on time."

"Right—interesting—I know—can you just hurry it up?" Liam asked.

"There's your change," Glenn said handing it back to Liam, "Have a nice weekend."

"Yeah, thanks," Liam said as they all ran outside.

As they ran outside Liam handed six quarters down to Gabe who was sitting on the ground.

"Thank you, Liam. Have a nice weekend, boys," Gabe said.

Liam nodded as he ran over and hopped on to his bicycle and began pedaling slowly.

Once everyone was on their bicycles they saw a group of kids coming their way on bikes.

"They're here!" yelled Johnny as he began to pedal faster towards his house, "Come on!"

Although they all continued to pedal as fast as possible, the kids were more athletic and faster than them, even on bikes.

They were almost to their houses when they turned the corner into their neighborhood to see Ricky and Will standing at the entrance blocking their way in the distance. They were both on their bicycles ready for a chase as Johnny, Jack, and Liam stopped. They were trapped, cornered, sandwiched—there was no way out.

"We're so screwed," Jack said as he looked around.

"You've gotta be shi—" Johnny was cut-off.

"There!" Liam pointed to their right. It was another road that branched off and out of their neighborhood and toward the woods. Granted it would get them farther away from their houses, but they might be able to lose them deep in the woods.

Unfortunately, the woods would take about forty-five to sixty minutes to reach and was about fifteen miles away. Liam, Johnny, and Jack did know the woods like the back of their hands after all.

All three of them immediately turned right and started to ride toward the woods as fast as possible.

"GO, GO, GO!" Ricky yelled as he started to pedal towards them with Will. The group of kids that followed was only a group of around ten or so people that had only agreed to chasing Jack, Johnny, and Liam down so they could go to Will's party that started later that night.

It didn't take as long as it usually did for Jack, Johnny, and Liam to get to the entrance to the woods. They were going faster than normal to escape their tormentors as they pedaled their hearts out. Dirt trails and trees surrounded them, which would make it hard for Will and Ricky to spot them.

"We should ditch our bikes," Liam said hopping off of his, "so we can run into the woods where the bikes can't fit."

Nobody argued as they each hopped off of their bikes and ran into the more heavily wooded area. As they continued to run Johnny started to wheeze and started to slow down. He quickly pulled out his asthma container and breathed it in.

"Hurry!" Jack said as Johnny stuck his container back into his pocket and continued to run.

Far behind them they could hear Ricky and Will talking to one another.

"Looks like they ditched their bikes," Ricky said.

"They must've gone into the woods where bikes can't follow them," Will said as he started to head into the woods along with Ricky. All the other athletic guys weren't talking, but Jack, Johnny, and Liam could tell that they were right behind following Ricky and Will as well.

"Our best chance is to hide," Liam said continuing to run, "Because we definitely can't outrun, outfight, or outlast them—but we can hide from them."

"Agreed," Jack and Johnny said in sync as they cut left and ran deeper into the woods. Finally, after minutes of running, they stopped when they felt that they had ran far enough. They hid behind some big trees and tried to steady their breathing as they waited to see if Will or Ricky would show up.

It took a few minutes, but soon footsteps could be heard creeping through the woods. It must've been Ricky and Will.

Jack, Johnny, and Liam tried to remain as quiet as possible as the footsteps grew louder and louder.

Finally, once the footsteps were practically right next to them, Liam jumped out from behind a tree as he held up his fists. Once Will's face came into view Liam swung with all his might right at the nose. His swung missed by a whole foot as it swiped through the air.

"Run!" yelled Liam. As he ran Will grabbed the plastic bag with the comic book in it, ripping it out of Liam's grip. "No!" Liam turned around to see Will pulling the comic book out of the plastic bag.

"Liam, come on!" yelled Johnny, "We can get a new comic book, it's fine!"

Liam didn't care. It wasn't about the comic book anymore. It was about pride. This harassment wouldn't stop until Liam took a stand.

"Give it back," Liam said tightening his fists, his knuckles turning white.

Will bit his lip as he thought for a second and said, "Give what back?" He was now opening up the comic book and flipping through the pages.

"Now," Liam demanded.

Will squinted as he tilted his head and looked at Liam, "Or what?"

Liam swung as hard as he could. Will's face was right in front of him and would be an easy target to hit if he could just time it perfectly. Unfortunately, Liam wasn't the most athletic person or strongest person, so he missed. Not by a lot—he actually came pretty close—but it only made Will angrier.

As Liam's fist swept through the air in front of him, Will grabbed the first page of the comic book and ripped it out.

R

I

P

"No!" Liam yelled out as Will crumpled the page into a ball and threw it to the ground of the woods.

"Now, here's how this is going to wor—" Will was interrupted.

"Why are you doing this, Will? Why do you hate us? What did we ever do to you?" Liam asked, cutting Will off.

Will pursed his lips together and grabbed the next page in his hand, ready to tear it, "I don't like being interrupted.

R

I

P

"Will, come on! Stop!" Liam yelled out on the verge of tears.

"Like I said—this is how it's going to work," Will continued, "You and weasel over there are going to walk away and leave nerd behind."

"What? Why?" asked Liam.

"Because word has gotten around that nerd has a crush on Ricky's girlfriend, and if we just let people go around and plot and think about how to steal someone's girlfriend where would we be?" Will said it so fast it was almost inaudible. Everyone just looked at him blankly for a few seconds. "Okay," Will continued, "Nerd and Ricky have some private business to take care of involving Samantha."

"What? Dude?" Liam asked, "It's just a joke. He doesn't even like her." He was willing to do anything to get out of this mess.

"Well, prove it," Will said, "If nerd here is willing to get a good punch to the face then we'll leave you all alone and this whole thing will be dealt with."

"Are you serious?" asked Johnny.

"Dude, it's fine," Ricky said, "Just let them off with a warning. They're already scared enough as it is."

Will looked at Ricky with a strange look on his face, "Now, now, Ricky—what type of example would I be setting if I didn't give them some form of physical punishment?"

"Dude, she's my girlfriend—it's fine. Leave them alone," Ricky said.

"And now you refuse to stand up for your girlfriend?" Will asked. "You know, it always was a shame how spineless you were," Will paused and then looked up at Liam, Johnny, and Jack. "Send nerd up."

"No," Liam said. He wasn't going to let his friend get punched for having a stupid crush on someone.

"What did you just say to me?" Will declared, tightening his fist.

"I said, NO!" Liam yelled.

"Dude—he said no," Ricky said holding Will back.

Will stood there for a while as he clenched his jaw in anger. It was silent for about ten seconds until Will said, "Get off me, man," and pushed Ricky's restraining arms off of him and turned around as he started to walk away. "Oh, and the comic," Will turned around and held it up as he ripped it in half, "Have fun reading it."

R

I

P

Jack, Johnny, and Liam stood there as they watched Will, Ricky, and the rest of the group walk away towards the exit of the woods as the ripped comic book pages blew away in the subtle breeze that worked its way through the trees.

       The bell dangling in front of the door *jingled* as Liam threw it open and rushed to the counter. Jack and Johnny were right behind him as they walked up to the front desk. Glenn was nowhere to be found. Carol was in the comic store standing next to a shelf with awe as Liam stood there in front of the desk. Liam had noticed her out of the corner of his eye but this would be one of the few rare instances where he wouldn't care. This would also be one of the few rare instances where Johnny and Jack wouldn't make kissing noises whenever he was around Carol. It just wasn't the right time for something like that.

       On top of the desk was a silver bell that laid there motionless waiting to be *rung*. However, though it would've been the easiest solution, Liam refused to ring the bell and instead he brought his fist down onto the counter with a loud *crash*. The *crash* echoed throughout the tiny comic store as Glenn came walking to the front counter to see what all of the commotion was about. Once he arrived out of his back workspace he was greeted by Liam, Johnny, and Jack standing there fuming with anger and tearing up with sadness. So far, no tears had been shed, but their bloodshot eyes told the truth of their pain.

       "Hey, guys," Glenn continued as his eyebrows scrunched up in confusion, "What's wrong?" He sounded more distressed than angry, however, if it were anyone but Liam, Johnny, and Jack that had banged his counter he would've been angry.

Liam didn't answer as he slowly opened his fist that had slammed against the counter. As he opened his fist little crumpled up pages of comic books spilled out onto the counter. Not all of them were there, just the few that they managed to get before the rest of them blew away in the wind.

Glenn pursed his lips. He didn't even have to unfold the crumpled comic book pages to know what happened as he let out a slight sigh of sadness. Not anger; not annoyance; not disappointment, but sadness. He wasn't even the least bit angry with them.

"Come with me, Liam," Glenn said as he motioned with his hand for Liam to walk behind the counter. Liam did as he was told. He didn't ask any questions—he didn't even care that Glenn was taking him into the forbidden backroom of the comic store. It hadn't even crossed his mind.

The back room had always been something that the three friends joked about with each other. *"I wonder what's back there."* and *"I bet it holds all of Glenn's secrets."* so when Liam was able to go back there with Glenn, it was a pretty big deal.

"W-what about us?" Johnny asked, desperate to see what was in the back room for himself.

Glenn looked at them as he shrugged, "I dunno. Go hang or something," and with that he walked Liam to the back room of the comic shop.

Silence filled the store of the comic shop as Carol continued to stare in awe and in confusion.

"I swear if Liam doesn't tell us what's back there I'm gonna—" Johnny was cut off.

"You're gonna what?" asked Jack, "Get us chased down by Ricky Jason and Will Tucker and nearly get the crap knocked out of us?"

Johnny squinted as his eyebrows scrunched up. "You think this is my fault?" he laughed.

"Uh, yeah!" yelled Jack, "If you hadn't gone around school yellin' about how I had a stupid crush on Samantha they wouldn't have chased us down in the first place!"

"Dude, they probably already knew that you had a stupid crush on Samantha!" yelled Johnny as he pointed at Jack.

"Then why the heck would they choose to come after us on the one day that you go blabbing about it to everyone?" Jack angrily asked, his face turning bright red.

"Heck if I know—but this is hardly my friggin' fault!" Johnny yelled, "It's like you just want someone to blame it on so you don't feel bad about almost getting us beaten up!"

"Why would I feel bad?" Jack screamed, "I can't control my feelings I have for Samantha! I can't control what my heart feels!"

"A—" Johnny stumbled over words as he stopped. He couldn't think of anything else to say. No more comebacks—which he was usually good at— and no more arguing. "I'm at a loss for words," was all he could muster.

"Yeah, I can see that!" Jack yelled as he turned around and stormed out of the front door of the comic shop.

"Jack, wait!" Johnny yelled as he ran outside toward Jack as the bell *jingled* overhead.

"Get away from me," Jack said as he walked over to his bicycle in the bicycle rack and hopped on it, "And tell Liam once he's done, he'll know where to find me."

"Your house?"

"W—no—just—just tell him that he'll know where to find me!" Jack said angrily as he started to ride towards his house a few blocks away.

"Sounds like somethin's wrong there," said Gabe sitting behind Johnny against the comic shop wall.

Johnny sighed, "No kidding."

"You guys also seemed kinda upset when you walked into the store—or Liam did at least," Gabe continued as Johnny stood there, back still turned to him, as he continued to watch Jack ride away. "Wanna talk about it?"

Johnny paused and then shook his head, "No."

"Okay," Gabe continued, "Now how 'bout the truth? Would you like to talk about it?"

Johnny paused again, "You know, Gabe," Johnny turned around and walked over to him as he sat against the comic book store brick wall next to Gabe, the shade shielding them from the sun, "For someone who's unemployed you're pretty friggin' smart."

Gabe chuckled, "Why thank you, kind sir. So, what exactly happened?"

"Well, you see, it is my fault," Johnny said, "I mean, looking back I kinda see how it's my fault."

"Hmm," Gabe thought, "Continue."

"There's this girl at school—"

"There always is," Gabe pointed out as he smiled.

"And Jack likes her, however, one of the popular kids at school is already dating her and I told everyone that Jack liked her."

"I see."

"Well, eventually the word got around to Ricky and Will and all of their buddies and they followed us from school. We out-rode them to the woods so we could hide, but they ended up finding us. When they did I thought that they were going to beat the sh—"

"Crap," Gabe corrected.

"Out of us. Thankfully all they did was rip up our comic that we had just bought. If it weren't for Ricky, who told Will to leave us alone, we'd be goners for sure."

"Okay, I understand," Gabe continued, "but if you're not hurt and nobody else got hurt, then what are you all so upset and worked up about?"

"They humiliated us. They made us feel weak and just in general scared us to death. It wasn't as much of a fight as it was a threat," Johnny said.

"So, Jack's upset because you almost got the crap beaten out of you guys?" Gabe asked.

"Yeah."

"Well, it is partially your fault, but it's nothing to get worked up about," Gabe continued. "Give it a day or two—he won't be able to stay mad at you forever."

Johnny moved his lips to the left side of his mouth as he thought. "Thanks, Gabe," he finally said as he stood up and walked towards the entrance of the store, "I can always count on you."

Johnny quickly walked into the comic shop and toward the front counter. On the counter remained the crumpled balls of comic pages. He quickly snagged them up and stuffed them into his pockets and quickly walked back outside.

Johnny walked over to the bike rack. Before he left he shot Gabe a quick glance, "Oh, and," he continued, "if Liam asks, he knows where to find Jack."

Gabe smirked, "Okay."

And with that Johnny rode off, not to his house, not to Jack's house, but the woods.

"What happened?" Glenn asked, full of distress. They were in the back room of the comic store, and it was a pretty big deal, but that hardly seemed important to Liam. However, if Liam wasn't so preoccupied with being upset and humiliated about this whole situation he probably would've found it underwhelming. No secrets; no entertainment; And, regretfully, nothing inappropriate for a kid under 18. It was just a four-cornered white walled everyday room with a few comic and movie posters hung on the wall. So disappointing.

"I-I don't know," Liam said, his red dreary eyes full of tears, as he gasped after he said a word.

"Okay; okay—calm down—everything's fine," Glenn said grabbing Liam by the shoulders as he bent down so he was face-to-face with him. "Wipe those tears away."

Liam wiped the tears running down his face with the back of his hand as he tried to calm down. He took deep, steady breaths, trying to maintain his composure. After a few seconds of deep breaths Liam managed to calm down, and right when he did he looked around to check his surroundings and soon with bulging eyes he said, "Hey! We're in the back room of the comic store!"

A grin stretched to the right side of Glenn's face as he nodded, "Yep," he chuckled, "You're definitely the first besides me."

"Really?"

Glenn nodded, "Little disappointing, right?" He looked around along with Liam. The white walls—well most of them at least—were painfully blank and empty and plain, but a couple of them looked pretty good with the posters hung on them.

"No 18+ stuff like we thought," Liam said, his eyes still red and he was still continuing to calm down. He too had a slight grin on his face, for he knew that Jack and Johnny would just be dying to know what was back there, and he knew that he was going to refuse to tell them. It would kill them.

"No," Glenn paused, "I keep that stuff in the other back room."

"What?" Liam asked, intrigued.

"I'm just kidding," Glenn said giving Liam a hug. "You okay?" he asked.

Liam nodded, "I will be."

"So, you wanna tell me what happened?" Glenn inquired.

Liam shook his head, "I think I'll be fine."

"And do I need to call anyone's parents, have a little chat—maybe let your mom get involved?" Glenn asked, though he already knew the answer to his question.

"Please, for the love of God, no," Liam chuckled, "The last thing I want is for my mom going up to the school and filing a huge complaint about this whole situation—she has enough to worry about as it is."

Glenn nodded, unwrapping his arms from around Liam and running his hands through Liam's hair, messing it up. "Let's go," he smiled.

"Wait, is Carol still out there?" Liam asked, stopping in his tracks.

"Carol?"

"That girl."

"Oh," Glenn smirked, "*That* girl."

"Shut up!" Liam yelled.

"I see what's goin' on here."

Liam scrunched up his eyebrows as he pointed at Glenn, "You better not say anything to her—I know she's a regular customer, and I swear if you so much as even talk about me with her—"

"Whoa! Calm down," Glenn said chuckling, "I won't tell her—your secret's safe with me."

"Okay, well can you at least take a peek, see if she's still out there?" Liam asked.

Glenn nodded as he walked out the door. He was gone for a good five seconds before re-entering the back room. "She's still there."

"Okay," Liam sniffled as he rubbed his eyes, "I can't let her see me like this."

"Like what?" Glenn asked, "You look fine."

"My eyes are blood-red!" Liam stated, "If I go out there like this then she'll know that I've been crying!"

"Fine," Glenn said, "What do you want me to do?"

"Well, can we just wait until my eye aren't red anymore and then leave?" Liam pleaded.

"Okay," Glenn sighed, "But I'm goin' out to the counter where I have customers that need my attention, and whenever you're ready you can come on out."

Liam nodded, "Copy that." Glenn walked out and stood behind the front desk as he turned to Carol. She was still standing in the same area that she was before.

"You know if you want to read that you could always buy it," Glenn said leaning against the counter.

"It's fine," Carol said, "I'm not really a collector, I just like reading the stories."

"You know—it's people like you that are goin' to put me outta business," Glenn joked.

Carol chuckled, "Yeah."

"What comic you got?" asked Glenn.

"Secret Wars—just came out. I'm enjoying it so far, but I just wonder how long that this series could last. It may kind of screw up the chronology of the Marvel comic timeline."

"I'm sorry?" Glenn asked.

"It's just—the story is amazing, don't get me wrong—but I'm afraid that having different heroes from different series in the same comic series might make the timeline of the events in which things happen hard to keep up with."

Glenn raised an eyebrow, "I see what you're sayin', but I kinda like the idea."

"I do to," Carol continued, "I just—I hope that they don't screw it up."

Glenn nodded, "Yeah, me to." As Glenn said that Liam walked through the door to the back room and into the main comic area. He was about to walk out of the store when Glenn said, "Hey, Liam," Liam turned around and looked at Glenn without saying a word, "Would you like another Secret Wars issue. I'll give one to you for free since your other one got torn up." Liam refused to talk, startled by how he was so suddenly put on the spot. "Oh, also, this is Carol," Glenn said pointing to Carol, "And she's actually reading Secret Wars right now."

Carol waved as Liam said, "Yeah, I think we go to the same school," he was obviously playing dumb, as if he didn't already know they went to the same school.

Carol nodded, "Yeah, we have the same history class."

"Well, Carol was just telling me how she liked the Secret Wars comic, but how she's also somewhat worried about it," Glenn said, bringing up new topics so the conversation would continue and not become awkward and dull.

"Worry about it—why?" asked Liam, slowly inching his way closer to Carol who was on the other side of the store.

"Well, it might make the timeline a little too confusing," she pointed out as she closed the comic book that she was holding and set it back on the shelf.

"Yeah, I see what you're saying!" Liam agreed. "But I feel like if the creators execute the idea just right and in a certain way that it could be revolutionary."

"Oh, I totally agree," Carol continued. "It will be a risk—could be for the better; could be for the worse. We'll just have to wait and see."

Liam nodded as Glenn butted in again, "You know," he continued, "My favorite comics are probably some from the X-Men."

"What issue, though—that's the real question," Carol said pointing at Glenn.

"None in particular," he shook his head, "I really just love the series as a whole."

Carol nodded in agreement as Liam said, "I can't choose. I really just like almost every comic that I read and I can't imagine having to pick between them."

Carol's eyes widened as she said, "Same!" She pointed at Liam. Pointing at people whenever she talked to them was probably just her thing though. "I love so many comics that I would never be able to pick between them."

Liam nodded as silence fell upon them until finally Liam said, "Well, I better get goin'. It's gonna get dark soon and my mom's gonna be worried sick if I'm not home in time for dinner."

"Well, see ya' Monday," Carol said as Liam walked toward the door.

"See ya."

"Would you like that Secret Wars issue refund now, Liam?" Glenn asked before he walked out of the shop.

"No, it's fine. Just give it to Carol," Liam said as he walked out and waved to Glenn. Once Liam walked out of the comic shop a cool breeze hit him as the sun set in the horizon. As he walked to his bike he smiled to himself.

"Hey, Liam!" Gabe yelled.

Liam walked right past Gabe on his way out of the comic shop. He didn't even see him there. "Hey, Gabe! What's up?"

"Oh, nothin'," Gabe continued, "Johnny just told me to tell you that Jack said that you would know where to find him."

"What?" Liam asked, hopping onto his bike, getting ready to leave.

"Oh, never mind." Gabe was too old for this crap. "You know where to find Jack."

"Oh, okay," Liam said, "Thanks, Gabe." With that Liam rode away as he waved goodbye to Gabe and Gabe waved back.

"Good night!" Gabe yelled, but Liam was already gone.

"How irresponsible, Johnny, for you to stay out this late—I thought you knew better, Johnny—Well it seems that you are gonna have to be punished—We specifically told you to be home by dinner time, and you disobeyed us!" Johnny mocked his parents as he threw his bike to the ground. It was almost dark, and the sun was setting, which meant Johnny didn't have a lot of time to do what he wanted without having to go back to his house and get a flashlight. But he couldn't do that, because then his parents would make him stay home. They didn't understand. They almost never understood.

Johnny quickly ran into the woods and back to the spot where they had a close encounter with Ricky, Will, and the rest of their friends. Once he reached the area he pulled out his asthmas container and sucked it in as he refreshed his lungs. He stood where they had stood earlier that day and looked around him. There wasn't much there but Johnny did catch something out of the corner of his eye. He quickly ran toward the comic page that was gently swaying in the wind and grabbed it. Once he captured the page he looked at the page number and shoved it into his pocket. He then proceeded to pull out a small notepad that was in his other pocket with a list of numbers on it. He marked off 13 and 14 on the pad of numbers 1-26. Along with 13 and 14 crossed off the list 1 and 2—7 and 8—11 and 12 were all also crossed off the list. Although there were 26 pages worth of comic book—counting front and back as 2—he wasn't counting the title page. That should be the easiest to find just because it was the most colorful and the thickest, so it shouldn't have been blown as hard as the thinner pages.

Johnny searched for hours and hours, and soon it was dark out. The mosquitos were nipping at his neck and arms and he only had 2 more pages to go…. 3 and 4—5 and 6. He had already found the title page and by now his pocket was overflowing with comic book pages, but he would have to push through. Thankfully it wasn't too hot or humid outside like most nights when it became close to summer. It was a nice cool night and the breeze sent a chill up Johnny's spin.

Once Johnny had finally found the last two pages, he ran out of the wooded brush and picked up his bike that he had thrown down earlier. He hopped on to it and rode out of the woods.

He knew he would be in big time trouble with his parents, but it would be worth it. Well worth it. It took a good thirty minutes to get to his house—he made good time—and he pulled his bike up the driveway as he walked up to his front door. He tried to open it but it was locked. Thankfully the house key was underneath the mat outside like always.

Once Johnny walked into his house and placed the key back under the rug, everyone was asleep. Johnny ever so quietly closed the door.

C

    R

        E

            A

                K!

Johnny winced as he tip-toed inside his room. Once he made it to his room he closed the door behind him and sat down at his desk. On his desk was a lamp, a stapler, a blank notebook, and a pencil and a few pens in a coffee mug. He quickly pulled out all of the crumpled-up pages of the comic book and lined them up in chronological order. After he had them all in the right order, he stacked them on top of each other and he stapled them together.

Good as new...

Kinda.

Johnny flipped to the back of the title page and got a pen and started to write something on the inside cover. Once he was done he put his pen back into the coffee mug.

C
    L
       I
         N
           K!

Johnny grabbed the crumpled pages that were stapled together and walked out of his room. He quietly closed the door behind him as he proceeded toward the front door of his house. Once he reached the front door he unlocked it.

C
    L
       I
         C
          K!

He opened the door.

C
    R
       E
         A
          K!

He quickly stepped outside into the night air as he closed the door behind him.

C
    R
       E
         A
          K!

When he was sure that he was in the clear he ran to his bicycle and hopped onto it as he rode toward Jack's house.

The night air pressed against Johnny's face causing him to blink more than usual. He rode on the right-side of the road because it was night and he didn't want to get hit by a moving car. At least this way the car would be able to see him before it hit him or something. The blue moonlight glowed onto the street in front of Johnny as he continued to ride toward Jack's house.

Finally, when Johnny had made it to Jack's house, he sat down his bike and walked up to the front door. He stood there at the front door for about thirty seconds before setting the comic book pages stapled together on the ground in front of his door. He wasn't sure how Jack would react to this—much less his parents—he was kinda waking them up in the middle of the night after all.

Johnny, without any more hesitation, rang the doorbell. He heard it echo through the whole house before he ran, picked up his bike, and zoomed off down the street.

As Johnny zoomed off he could hear the front door of Jack's house opening, and Johnny smiled as he rode home.

Liam and Jack sat upstairs in Jack's room as they talked. Even though Jack was upset, Liam didn't seem nearly as upset as him. In fact, Liam wasn't even bothered by this whole situation. He knew that this whole thing would just brush over in a few weeks or so.

"I mean, I can't believe Johnny would do something like that," Jack said as he paced back and forth at the foot of his bed.

Liam was sitting there watching Jack as he said, "It's not really a big deal."

Jack was shocked, "Not a big de—"

"And it's not Johnny's fault either," Liam stated.

"It is though!" Jack yelled, "How can you not see that this is his fault?"

Liam shrugged, "I think it's my fault. If I didn't let Ricky sit with us and if I had listened to you guys about it being a trap, then we wouldn't have gotten in this mess anyway. And besides, how was Johnny supposed to know that Ricky, Will, and the rest of their group would come after us because of a stupid crush you have?"

Jack squinted as he thought long and hard. He stood there motionless as he pulled off his big, thick, round glasses and set them on a desk. They *clanked* against the wooden desk as Jack grabbed the upper part of his nose with two fingers as if he had a headache.

"Now that I think about it, it probably wasn't even about your crush on Samantha," Liam suggested, remaining calm as Jack was stressing out.

"What do you mean?" Jack asked, "Why else would they even want to pick on us?"

"Open your eyes, Jack," Liam continued, "They've always picked on us—this is just the first time that it's come close to getting physical. They probably just told us that that was the reason so they would have something to fall back on just in case one of them threw a punch."

Jack remained silent as he picked up his glasses from the desk and put them back on his head, tucked sturdily behind his ears.

"What can I say," Liam continued, "Sometimes the strong like to take from the weak, but what they don't know is that the smart take from the strong, as well," Liam smiled slyly.

"But they don't even need a reason to beat us up, so why would they go to the trouble to make one up?" Jack asked.

Liam shrugged, "Maybe they wanted to be able to brag about how they beat you up because you liked Samantha. Maybe Samantha would find it romantic or at the very least some other girl would like Ricky because they would know that he would be able to protect her."

"Possibly, but what's the point?" asked Jack, "They already have Samantha, and she likes Ricky back. What more does he have to prove?"

Liam shrugged again, "Dude, I have no idea. Maybe they just thought that it would be fun to beat us up, pick on us, and tease you about your little crush all at once."

D

I

N

G!

"That's the doorbell," Jack said as turned around and walked out of his room.

As Jack walked toward the front door he heard his mom yell, "Jack, it's for you!"

Jack hurried toward the door even faster, his footsteps echoing down the hall, as he came to a stop at the door. In the doorway was a comic book. It was very torn up and staples were sticking out in every direction.

Jack stared in awe as he looked down at the comic book. Liam walked up behind Jack.

"Who's it from?" Liam questioned.

"I think it's from Johnny."

"Well, pick it up," Liam demanded.

"I'll just go," Jack's mom said as she walked away from the front door. The night air was slowly invading their house the longer they kept the door open as a gust of wind sent a chill up Jack's spine. "Be sure to close the door behind you," his mom continued, "and don't stay up too late." Her skin was really pale. Her eyes had sunken deep into her face and she always looked tired. Her voice trailed off in the distance.

"Yes, mom," Jack said as he bent down to pick up the comic book.

"Goodnight, Liam," Jack's mom said waving to him as she walked toward her bedroom.

"Goodnight, Mrs. Simons." Liam replied as Jack bent down and picked up the comic book. "Dude," Liam started, "is your mom okay? She looks really tired and pale."

"Y-yeah. She just hasn't been feeling good recently," Jack said as he held it in his hands for a good thirty seconds before actually opening it up to the front page. "It's from Johnny," he paused as a smirk spread across his face. "He must've collected all of the pages from the woods and stapled them together."

"What does it say?" asked Liam.

"It says: **from johnny. ive been up most of the night collecting these pages for you piece of crap. and i hope you know that im stickin my neck out for you so you better apreciate this! im probably gonna be grounded cause of you.**" Jack looked up at Liam who was now smiling. "Wipe that grin off your face you idiot! If he really cared he would've used proper spelling and grammar in his letter."

Liam smiled even more, getting Jack's sarcasm. "You know, sometimes it's better to just appreciate the gesture."

"Heck, he must not think of himself very highly. He didn't even capitalize his name!" Jack stated sarcastically.

Liam started to laugh, "Come on, let's go to your room so we can read the comic before it's time to go to bed."

"Yeah," Jack agreed as they both walked down the hall to Jack's bedroom.

They stayed up the rest of that night reading the comic and talking to each other. They talked about comics, girls, and school. But most importantly, summer break. Boy, were they excited for summer break. It was the prize—award—for completing another school year without managing to fail any of their classes. Not to mention it meant a full three months of nothing but comics, exploring the woods, and fishing. It was a strange thing—fishing—for the three of them—Jack, Liam, and Johnny, that was—Jack and Johnny hadn't liked fishing until Liam introduced them to it. Liam never really seemed like a kid to enjoy fishing, but he did; oh boy, he did. Last summer break was when he brought Jack and Johnny to his famous fishing spot. It was on the railroad bridge that stretched across the lake where he liked to fish. He would sit on the very edge of the bridge and lean back and relax as he waited to catch a big one. Of course, Liam was a smart kid—smarter than most—and he never went out to sit in the middle of the bridge. He had always sat right on the edge where he could easily avoid a train if one were to come. The last thing he wanted was to be stuck on the middle of the tracks when a train would come and he would be forced to jump into the lake. Liam had always told himself that it wasn't a long drop or fall, but it was. Some of Liam's best memories were sitting on top of the rusted metal track that stretched across Lake Texoma. It was where he caught his first fish and where he brought his friends to enjoy a nice hot summer afternoon together. None of his friends had a boat to go down into the lake, so that was a bust, but they could always just go to a nearby beach and swim around.

And as Jack and Liam continued to talk, sleep soon fell upon them.

May 12, 1984

Chapter 2

Cap'n Cosmo

D

I

N

G!

Johnny's doorbell rang as the sound of Saturday morning chatter broke out through his house. His mom and dad were already awake and drinking morning coffee as Johnny ran toward the door.

"Who is it?" asked Johnny's dad as Johnny peered through the peep-hole. It was Jack and Liam wearing backpacks full of fishing rods. They probably had bait tucked away somewhere.

"Jack and Liam," Johnny replied as he opened the front door. He had somehow managed to get his parents to forget about his absence last night and they had no idea where he had been. It was something quite marvelous, actually. A stunt only the bravest and daring could accomplish without getting grounded for a whole month. Johnny was actually pretty proud of himself.

A gust of morning dew sprayed Johnny's face as he opened the door. He had just woken up and gotten dressed when the doorbell rang. He knew that it was probably Jack and Liam. They usually went fishing every Saturday—despite the few occasional absences of someone—and Johnny was usually ready to go right when his friends got there.

Jack was holding the comic book that Johnny had stapled back together once he opened the door. "Come on, slowpoke," Jack shoved the comic book into Johnny's chest as he snatched it up. "It's supposed to be one of the hottest days this year yet, so I'd get some water."

"Meet me out front," Johnny smiled as he stuffed the comic book into his bag.

They each had individual items that they were supposed to carry for Saturday fishing. Liam was in charge of the fishing rods; Jack was in charge of the bait; Johnny was in charge of comic books, and basically any other item of entertainment that you could possibly think of. Johnny was there basically to make sure that nobody got bored while fishing. Not to mention sunburned.

Johnny ran to his backyard where he kept his bike. He hopped on and road back around to the front yard. "Mom, dad! I'm goin' fishin' with Liam and Jack!"

"Have fun," his mom said plainly.

His dad didn't reply.

Johnny hopped on his bike in his backyard and circled back around to the front where Jack and Liam were waiting.

"I see you got my note," Johnny smiled proudly, as if he had accomplished something.

"Yeah," Jack continued, "You might wanna check your spelling," he paused, "and grammar." Jack took off down the street as the chains *popped* and *clicked* with every pedal.

"It's the thought that counts!" yelled Johnny as he chased back after Jack. Liam rode up front next to Jack as Johnny continued to catch up.

"Well, apparently you didn't *thought* anything," Jack said sarcastically.

Liam started to laugh, "Come on, guys. Let's get goin'. We wanna get there before it gets too hot. Don't wanna tire ourselves out too much from the heat by riding our bikes."

Johnny and Jack nodded in agreement as they picked up the pace a little.

"So, tell me this," Johnny continued, now riding right next to Jack and Liam. "Did you at least like the issue?"

Jack shrugged as the wind blew through his hair, the sun slowly rising over the pink horizon. "I think the series has potential."

"Yeah," Liam continued, "I wouldn't say it was amazing, but they could definitely make it work if it's done correctly."

"Well, I haven't read it yet," Johnny confessed. "So, don't spoil it!"

Liam started chuckling, "You better read it before Jack gets mad at you again."

"Yeah, tell me about it," Johnny smiled. "I plan on reading it once we get to the bridge."

"So, you guys got any plans for summer?" asked Jack. They all continued to pedal their bikes as they sped down the road. Even though they had only been riding their bikes for a few seconds it was already heating up outside.

Johnny and Liam shrugged as they simultaneously said, "Well—" They both stopped as they looked at each other and chuckled.

"Jinx!" yelled Liam before Johnny had thought to do it.

"Cra—" Johnny was cut off.

"Hey—you better be quiet or else you'll owe me a soda," Liam cracked a smile.

Johnny rolled his eyes as he turned his focus back onto the road in front of them.

"Well," Liam continued, "not much. The only thing I really have goin' on is pretty much hangin' with you guys. Doin' lots of fishin'."

"Yeah," Jack continued, "I got nothin' planned. I am lookin' forward to it though."

"The heat will drive you crazy though," Liam stated.

Jack just nodded as they continued to ride down the road toward the woods. The woods were the first place they had to head, and then they would be able to easily find the train tracks that led to their favorite fishing spot.

As they continued to pedal their ever-loving hearts and souls out, houses and kids and people raced past them in a colorful blur of disarray. All of the houses that they passed by were old and torn up. If most people were to visit it for the first time then they would probably think that it was a bad, crime-filled part of town—but it wasn't. The houses were just old and weathered—so were most of the people—and it was just life for Johnny, Jack, and Liam now. They were surrounded by people of grandparenting age and lived close to only a few other kids that they were friends with. Of course, because it was such a small town, you lived close to everybody, but living close to everybody was sometimes a problem. Sometimes you didn't want to live close to everybody. Sometimes you didn't want to live next to the school bullies. Sometimes you didn't want to have to see them every day, even on the weekends. Heck, who did? But it was their way of life now. They had grown accustomed to it. And in that one small town that they lived in there was one comic store, one arcade, one or two restaurants, and just one school. All of the high schoolers and elementary students went to the same school. For the most part it wasn't all that bad. Most of the high schoolers would leave the younger kids alone, and most of the younger kids would refrain from being annoying to the older kids. However, there were the few cases where a high schooler would say something to one of his friends and a younger kid would just happen to be standing within ear-shot. That's when things got ugly. Whether the high schooler was cursing or talking about something inappropriate that no elementary kid should know about, it would get ugly... fast. Most of the times the principals would find out because—let's be honest—most young kids are some of the biggest snitches you will ever find or meet on the face of this earth. It's just a fact. And sometimes, if it's really bad, the parents would get involved. Maybe the young kid would repeat what the older kid said. It didn't matter. The parents would be completely enraged. But all of that was beside the fact and far away from everyone's mind as they headed toward the railroad bridge.

After about five minutes of riding Johnny yelled out, "Okay, I'll just give you a friggin' soda. It's not worth it."

"Okay," Liam continued, "I expect to get that soda by tomorrow."

"Tomorrow!?" yelled Johnny in shock.

Liam nodded as Jack said, "You heard the man. Tomorrow."

"No fair!" claimed Johnny.

"Hey," Jack shrugged, "It's part of the rules. Whoever jinxes someone, they get to choose when the soda is due."

"Just be happy I'm not making you get me a soda today," Liam pointed out.

"I may as well," Johnny said.

"What?" Liam asked, "Get me one today?"

"Yeah," Johnny continued, "I mean we're gonna stop by the gas station anyway on our way. I'll just buy one for me and one for you. I'll just get it over with."

"Nice!" Liam pumped his fist in the air, "Two sodas!"

"You better watch out now," Jack pointed out, "If you start havin' too many of those things you'll end up like Cap'n friggin' Cosmo o'er here."

Liam started laughing, and Johnny giggled like a baby in the background. Cosmo was his last name. They didn't know how they had figured this out, but it had just come by them one day so that's what they started to call him. Over time they had forgotten his first name which made it an even more ridiculous name for such a man but he didn't seem to mind it. Of course, he was completely oblivious of his size and that the kids were teasing him so why would he mind it?

"I'd expect as much from someone who's surrounded by coke all day in such a small store," Liam continued, "Heck, if I had nothing better to do with my life why not drink the sorrow away—with coke?"

"I just feel bad for Chipper," Johnny confessed, "Ol' thing's prob'ly dead by this week."

Chipper was the dog that Cosmo owned. It was sort of the store mascot and whenever the kids went inside Chipper would just groan. It was an old Golden Retriever and was just as fat as Cosmo. It had probably once been a healthy dog but ever since it had come to know Cosmo it had gotten fat with him as well.

"Cosmo's first love," Jack said sarcastically.

"Oh, no," Johnny continued, "his first love was most definitely food. Chipper comes in a not-so-close second."

"Chipper ate Cosmos's first love and then pinned it on the cat. That sly dog," Liam laughed.

"No," Jack said, "the cat's most definitely eaten by now."

"Are you kiddin'? It's been eaten!" Johnny burst out in laughter.

"At least the cat wasn't forced to be friends with Cosmo," Liam said.

"Oh, Chipper," Jack shook his head in disgust, "I wonder why you don't just leave that dump sometimes."

"That's what I'd do if I were Chipper," Johnny confessed.

"If I were Chipper I'd probably kill myself," Liam laughed.

"Here, here," Johnny acted as if he were raising a glass of wine as the three friends continued to ride down the road toward the woods.

After about five more minutes of speeding down the small road that went through Kingston, they reached the gas station. Those five minutes of pedaling had been full of silence and wind running through their hair. It was one of the many things that Liam enjoyed about hanging out with his friends, Jack and Johnny. Not only did they understand him, the things he liked and his sense of humor, but they too, like Liam, enjoyed the small moments that they got to savor in silence. Like the Saturday fishing trips they went on. Liam enjoyed those more than anything in the world. When Liam first moved to Kingston, he didn't have many friends. Not many people understood his liking for comics and certain 'nerdy' things. Not even his parents fully understood why he liked them so much. But before a couple days had passed at his new school, Jack and Johnny saw him reading a comic alone at lunch so they decided to go sit with him. That was how they all three met. Of course, that was a long time ago and the three of them have known each other and been best friends for about three years now; maybe more! But despite everything that has happened—every fight—every laugh—every tear—they have managed to remain best friends. It's the longest friendship that Liam had ever had and probably will ever have, for a friendship like this could last a lifetime.

D

I

N

G!

The two front glass doors to the gas station flung open as the three kids fumbled in. Although Chipper was out of sight they could hear his silent but fading *grumble* come from behind the counter where Cosmo was standing.

"Hey, Liam! Hey, Jack! Hey, Johnny!" Cosmo said as he always does when they entered the gas station.

"Hey, Cosmo," Liam said as he walked up to the counter and tried peeking over it where the soft *grumble* of Chipper came from. "Why isn't Chipper out front?" Liam was unable to see Chipper over the counter so he stood up straight and counted his losses as he looked up at Cosmo with curiosity.

"YEAH," Johnny's voice could be heard from the back of the gas station. "CHIPPER'S THE STORE MASCOT. HE'S GOTTA REPRESENT!"

"I don't know, guys," Cosmo's quiet, shy voice came from out of his huge body. It would be considered surprising at first to most people who heard his voice. "He's been really weird lately and I think he's just not feeling good."

"YO', LIAM!" Johnny yelled from the back of the store.

"WHAT!?" Liam yelled back turning his head around even though Johnny and Jack were both out of sight.

"WHAT FLAVOR YOU WANT!?"

"I DON'T WANT NO FLAVO'!" Liam yelled in a goofy slang talk. "I WANT DAT DR. PEPO, BOY; YOU KNOW HOW WE DO!"

"YOU GOT IT, BOSS!" Johnny yelled back across the store.

"What's that about?" asked Cosmo looking in Johnny's direction.

"I jinxed him."

"Ohhhh..." Cosmo stretched it out until it was worn thin and it dissipated into thin air as if nothing had ever been said.

"IS THAT ALL YOU WANT!?" Johnny yelled from across the store once again.

"WHAT!? YOU GONNA BUY ANOTHER THING FOR ME!? MR. GOOD SAMARITAN!" Not that he didn't already know the answer. Johnny obviously wasn't going to buy Liam anything else. He knew that Liam had brought his own money. Liam was just teasing Johnny a bit while he could.

"SONNY BOY, I'LL TELL YOU WHAT," Johnny continued as he walked to the front of the store. He got closer and closer to Liam and Cosmo, but that didn't stop him from not yelling. "MAYBE I WAS, BUT WITH THAT KINDA COMMENT YOU JUST LOST YO'SELF A SNACK." Johnny was now standing right next to Liam with two Dr. Peppers in his hands.

"BS!" claimed Liam. "You wouldn't have gotten me a snack if it were free!"

Johnny just shrugged, "Maybe not, but I guess now we'll never know."

"Oh, I know all right," Liam said playfully jabbing Johnny in the chest with his index finger.

"Would you two quit your jabbering," Jack said walking up to the counter. "I'm on the verge of killing myself—and to think I have a whole day left to spend with you guys." He shook his head in disappointment, refusing to make eye-contact with anyone.

Everyone set their items on the counter except for Liam. He didn't have anything to set on the counter. Johnny had already gotten him a soda.

"Liam, are you gonna get some food?" asked Jack raising an eyebrow. "You're gonna get hungry and I'm not sharing my sandwich with anyone." He set his ham sandwich, which was wrapped up tightly in a plastic bag, on the counter.

"Oh, yeah," Liam remembered as he quickly grabbed a sandwich off of the shelf and ran back to the counter. "Thanks for reminding me."

"What about you?" asked Cosmo, "You don't want a sandwich?" He pointed at Johnny.

Liam and Jack peered over at Johnny as they all three stood in front of the counter. Johnny just shrugged as he said, "Eh, I'll be fine."

"Okayyyy," Cosmo stretched the word out again. One of his many bad habits including his eating habits. "So that's two sandwiches, three Dr. Peppers and one Sprite."

Everyone nodded.

"That'll be $4.07."

Everybody paid for what they had gotten so it was a fair deal. Once they were finished, they walked out of the store as Chipper groaned again and Cosmo waved goodbye.

"Poor Chipper," Johnny made a sad face as he shook his head. "Why doesn't he just run away?"

Everyone tracked forth, determined to make it to Lake Texoma where they could fish all day long and hopefully bring home a hand full of deliciousness with them. The closer it got to summer the hotter it got and the harder it got for Johnny to keep up. Johnny has asthma. Obviously. And every summer he always has more trouble keeping up with Liam and Jack. However, they wait for him to regain his breath and continue on. This just happened to be the first day since last summer where Johnny had to stop to take a break. Everybody rode off to the side of the road and sat down in the yellow, crispy, dried up grass. They eventually found the perfect spot under a tree's shade to hang out for a while and talk.

"You okay, Johnny?" asked Liam, laying back in the not-so-soft grass as he looked up at the blue sky and tree limbs dangled above him.

"Yeah—I—just—need—a—break." He pulled out his inhaler as he quickly refreshed his lungs and let out a sigh of relief. "Man," he continued as he fell back into the grass next to Liam. "I love summer break, but I hate how hot it gets."

"Tell me about it," Jack agreed. He too was lying in the grass. They all were.

"Well, the swimming's not all that bad," Liam pointed out as a gust of wind blew his hair in his eyes as he smiled.

"Yeah, but we mean without the swimming. Like, when you're not in the lake having fun." Johnny said.

"Oh, well, if there's no swimming then yeah, I agree with you. But if swimming's in the picture it's not all that bad."

"Yeah," Jack continued, "I guess you're right. I am excited for the break, though."

"Oh, yeah!" Johnny smiled happily, "I love the three months of nothing but doing what you wanna do."

"It's right around the corner," Liam pointed out as he stretched his arms out and yawned.

"Does anyone know what time it is?" asked Jack.

Johnny and Liam both shook their heads.

"We just left like thirty minutes ago so it shouldn't be too late into the afternoon. Remember, we picked up Johnny around nine. Maybe ten at the latest," Liam suggested.

"It feels later than that, though," Jack said as he rubbed his grumbling stomach. "I'm already hungry for lunch."

"WHAT!?" yelled Johnny with surprise, "HOW!?"

Jack just shrugged as he started to laugh. "Bro, I'm always hungry."

And with that the three of them started to laugh as they laid in the dried up, yellow, crispy grass, the trees shielding the sun from their eyes.

"Well, then eat," Johnny suggested as he sat upright in the grass and watched as cars zoomed past them down the cracked road.

"Eh," Jack shrugged, "But then I'll be hungry later."

"I think I'm gonna drink one of my Dr. Peppers now. I have two anyway," Liam said as he sat upright in the grass and started to dig through the bag for a Dr. Pepper. He wrapped his hand around the cold glass bottle of Dr. Pepper and yanked it out of the big bag. Just looking at it made him thirsty. Liam quickly twisted the top off and threw it into his bag. The sizzle of the coke brought everyone to thirst as Liam took a small sip. He was going to savor this drink.

"Man, you know Sprite is my favorite drink, but just lookin' at that Dr. Pepper is makin' me thirsty," Jack licked his lips, his mouth feeling dryer than ever before. Much like a desert he felt dry. The sand was drowning him and soaking all of the liquid up from inside of him and replacing it with something else. Thirst. Thirst for a nice, crisp, cold, bottled soda to be running down his throat and washing away the huge desert that remained inside of him. "Ah, screw it," Jack said as he pulled out his Sprite, popped the cap open and let the rest work it's magic.

Johnny wasn't so easily manipulated or pressured, but he was pretty thirsty and a Dr. Pepper did sound good right about then. Soon they were all drinking sodas as they sat on the edge of the road, far enough away so they wouldn't get ran over but close enough to feel the *whoosh* of wind that came with each passing car.

"To Chipper," Johnny raised his bottle of Dr. Pepper in the air. "The most depressed dog in Kingston."

"And boy do we feel sorry for him," Liam smirked.

"Here, here," Jack said as he to raised his bottle of Sprite. And with that the three boys *clanked* their bottles of soda against each other as they continued on their way to Lake Texoma.

About five minutes after taking a break they made it to the entrance of the woods. The only reason Johnny hadn't needed to take a break when they were running away from Ricky and Will was because it wasn't nearly as hot then at night then it was now. It's much easier to ride a bike in cooler conditions than when it's around 90.F outside. That goes without saying though. Despite it all, they continued to ride their bikes into the entrance of the woods. It's located right off the main street and dips into a little valley. It's mostly covered up by trees and branches, so they had to push them aside to get through.

Once they were in the woods it was much cooler. The sweat that was dripping from everyone's head turned from hot and sticky to cold and crisp. It quickly cooled them off because the trees blocked the sun but still allowed wind to get through. Soon they were all cooled down and it was a much more relaxing ride. Johnny even sped up and caught up to Liam and Jack who had gotten ahead of him while riding to the woods.

The path the kids were riding on swerved in and out between trees as they slowed down to prevent falling off of their bike because they turned too sharp at such a high speed. Just because Liam could pull that stunt at the end of his street didn't mean he could do it in the woods. To their right was the lake. Lake Texoma to be more exact. From where they were they couldn't see the lake but they could smell the fresh moisture in the air and hear the small waves crashing on the shore. The seagulls squawked as they looked for fish that were on the surface of the water to snatch up.

They had tried once just to go straight to the sound of the water. They thought that it would be a quicker way to get to a beach and swim one summer. They were wrong. They had ridden their bikes toward the crashing waves, Jack maybe a little too fast, as they were prepared to jump into the nice refreshing lake water. Unfortunately, it was the side of a cliff that plummeted down into the waters with jagged edges poking out. There was no way down unless you were okay with your body being found in the lake several weeks later. That's why Jack was going a little *too* fast. Jack and Liam had no problem stopping their bikes in time as they peered over the edge of the cliff in awe, but Jack couldn't stop. He was headed straight off of the edge of the cliff and into the waters below. Liam and Johnny had tried to warn him before-hand but he didn't hear them. All he had heard was the *whooshing* of wind as he continued to pedal. Even their own voices sounded muffled to them as they yelled for Jack to stop. And in those few moments the change on Jack's face when he saw the cliff turned from excitement to pure terror. Not fear. He wasn't scared. He was full of pure terror. He pulled back his brakes as his tires slid against the dirt ground but he didn't stop. Much less slowed. He had only one option in those final moments. When he was about three feet away from the edge he jumped. He leapt off his bike as he yelled out for help and tears full of terror streamed down his face. Once he made impact upon the ground he began to roll toward the edge. It was nothing that Jack could've stopped. It would've been near impossible to stop rolling on his own because of the speed his bicycle—which now laid at the bottom of this cliff submerged in water—was going. He grabbed for dirt and twigs in the ground but just ended up pulling them up. Those moments where he was rolling felt as if they were in slow motion as he slid off the edge of the cliff. Thankfully Liam and Johnny had been there. Without them being there and grabbing him before he plummeted to his death—or without them acting so fast to the situation—Jack would've surely been a goner. Johnny and Liam were both lying on their stomachs, dirt covering Jack and their faces, as they held onto Jack's arms. Jack was halfway off the side of the cliff as he began to cry like a baby and he shook with—not fear—terror. Jack scraped his feet against the edge of the cliff as he tried to climb his way back up but to no avail. Johnny and Liam's grips were slipping from all of the sweat as Johnny, to, began to cry along with Jack. Liam, with all of the force he could muster, stood on both of his feet and pulled Jack up onto the side of the cliff. Johnny and Jack laid on their stomachs, scared out of their minds as they cried, and Liam sat down dazed, light-headed, in shock from what had just happened. His whole life he had thought himself to be immortal, but ever since that day he knew the true meaning of it all. Anyone can die at any moment. Whether that be because of a stupid mistake you made or a stupid mistake someone else made—it didn't matter. That was when the true possibility of dying had actually struck Liam. Not to mention Johnny and Jack. Jack is still scared about that day. Jack tells Liam and Johnny about the nightmares he has where he rolls off the side of the cliff but nobody catches him. He can't get close to ledges anymore. He can hardly stand fishing off of the edge of the railroad bridge. He was finally convinced that it was okay when Johnny and Liam told him that if you fell you would be fine because you would just fall in the water. But even so, why would you even jump or fall? Anyway, Jack and Johnny and Liam's stomachs were all bleeding because of how scraped they were, not to mention Jack's knees. They finally decided to go back home instead of swimming. They were all too bummed out anyway. They had trouble riding their bikes—Jack was sitting on the back of Liam's seat—and it was the longest 45 minutes that Liam had ever lived, but they made it back to their houses. Jack's parents were worried along with everyone else's parents. Of course, Jack, Johnny, and Liam didn't tell their parents what really happened, because if they did their parents wouldn't let them go into the woods anymore together. Instead they just told their parents that a drunk driver was driving on the wrong side of the road toward them and they all had to jump. They also mentioned Jack's bike getting ran over and snapped into pieces. It took about a month for anyone to regain the confidence of going back into the woods, but eventually they did. Now everything's back to normal. The only thing that's different is Jack's newfound fear of ledges.

"Welp, here it is," Liam said as he hopped off of his bike. In front of them was a narrow wooden railroad bridge that stretched over to Texas, and below it was Lake Texoma. Liam rolled his bike over to a nearby tree which he set his bike against as he walked over to the railroad bridge. Splintered pieces of wood stuck out in every direction and the metal tracks glowed in the summer light.

"Hey, guys," Johnny said as he set his bike against a different tree and opened up his backpack. Inside were several different comic books, a boom box, and two bottles of sun lotion. He held up the sunscreen and said, "don't wanna get burnt now do ya'?" He smirked as he handed Jack and Liam some sun lotion.

"Thanks," Liam said as he started to smear it across his face.

"Yeah, no problem. Just give me some once you're done puttin' it on," Johnny said as he zipped up his bag and walked over to the railroad bridge.

Liam slipped off his shirt and stuck it in the back of his shorts making it look like he had a tail as the blazing sun burnt his chest. He quickly smeared more lotion all over his chest and walked over to the train tracks where Johnny was already standing.

The railroad bridge didn't have any rails so if you fell you would plummet into the waters far down below. But that didn't stop the three boys. Why would they fall anyway?

They didn't walk too far out onto the railroad bridge in fear that a train would come by and they would have to jump. They stayed relatively close to the land where they could easily avoid the oncoming trains.

Liam sat his backpack down next to Johnny's as he sat down on the train tracks and dangled his legs off of the edge. The wood burnt his skin, but he didn't mind. It was actually kind of soothing once you got used to it.

Johnny stood up and slipped off his shirt as Liam handed him the sunscreen. Once everyone was covered in sun lotion, they all sat down on the edge of the bridge, shirtless, with their feet dangling.

Liam sat in the middle, like always, next to Johnny and Jack as he started to pull out three fishing rods that had been sticking out of his backpack all the way there. Jack got the bait out of his backpack and, as he and Liam prepared the fishing rods, Johnny pulled out his boombox and sat it next to him. He quickly turned it on and started to twist and turn the little knobs until he reached the station he was looking for. The boombox cut-on right in the middle of a song. None of them recognized it, but they enjoyed having something to listen to while fishing.

Liam handed Johnny his fishing rod with a worm attached to the end as Johnny cast it out into the lake below. Soon Liam and Jack did the same. And then they waited.

Johnny laid back onto the hot railroad tracks, nearly burning his back.

"AHH!" he called out in pain as he shot up. "That friggin' hurt!"

"Burn your back?" asked Liam.

Johnny nodded as he pulled his shirt out from the back of his pants and laid it down on the tracks behind him hoping that it would shield most of the heat from his back. He laid back and closed his eyes with a slight grin on his face.

"I love days like these," Johnny admitted. "Just be sure to wake me up if a train is comin' while I'm asleep."

Jack grinned, "Can't make any promises."

"Well, screw you Jack!" Johnny yelled out teasingly, his eyes still closed as he continued to smile. "I'm sure Liam's got my back."

"Yeah, about that—" Liam paused, refusing to finish his statement.

"Well—" he paused, "screw you to! Ya'll a buncho pieces of no-good father friggin' goody-two-shoes o'er here!"

Jack and Johnny quickly shot each other a confused glance as they both broke out in laughter. They were always shocked by the weird things that Johnny came up with.

"Are you gonna read the Secret Wars comic, Johnny?" asked Liam as he held his fishing pole between his legs with both of his hands.

"Later," he said.

"Are you tired or what?" asked Jack.

"Yeah, just tired," Johnny admitted.

"How are you tired?" asked Jack. "Are you like sleepy tired or physically tired?"

"Both, I guess—I don't know," Johnny continued. "Why're you askin' me hard-to-answer questions like that you no good—"

"Just curious," Jack interrupted.

"Well, can't a guy get some rest aroun' here without being bombarded and harassed by idiotic friends that he still hangs out with for some reason?" asked Johnny.

Liam raised an eyebrow and looked at Jack who just shrugged.

"Ya'know? I could totally make it better in school if I didn't hang out with a buncho dorks like you two," Johnny continued. "Maybe I could even sit at the table with Ricky and Will and all of their friends and be the guy pickin' on you two instead of bein' picked on *with* ya' two. Maybe even join the football team and become known as an athletic kid. You know—maybe even get Samantha Beasley."

"Screw you!" yelled Jack teasingly. "And for the record I would love to see ya' try'n pick'n us! We would totally just beat ya'up! Ain't that right-io, Liamio?"

"See," continued Johnny, "this is exactly why I'd beat ya'up! Who the heck says *right-io* anymore. Sounds pretty idiotic."

"Yeah," Liam continued. "We would totally beat up Johnny—but just for the record don't ever say *right-io* again."

Johnny started to laugh.

"Whatever," Jack shook his head somewhat embarrassed that he had said something so stupid and weird. That was usually Johnny's job.

"*Right-io, Liamo!*" Johnny mocked Jack as he remained lying down on the railroad tracks. "*While I'm on the subject-io why don't I just-io tell-io what-io I'm-io talkin-io about-io!*

"Idiot," Jack murmured under his breath. "You're so immature for someone whose older than me and Liam."

"Only by a couple months."

"Yeah, to Liam. But I'm a full year younger than you guys and I'm more mature than you," Jack claimed as he pointed in Johnny's direction.

"*Right-io, Jackio!*" Johnny yelled, confirming Jack's statement to be true.

"Screw you!" Jack laughed.

Johnny and Liam chuckled as they all continued to sit there, holding their fishing-rods, waiting for the fish to bite.

The sun blazed down on Jack, Johnny and Liam. If you would've been there with them you would've thought that the sun was scorching the earth by the minute, and you were soon to be another dust ball in the universe.

They all sat there, too hot to talk, as sweat dripped off of their foreheads and trickled down their backs. Johnny wasn't lying down anymore. He was sitting up with Liam and Jack now. It was around noon and they were all starting to get a little hungry.

"I'ma eat my sandwich," Jack said as he pulled his sandwich out of the bag.

"Yeah, me to," Liam said.

"Man, I'm hungry," Johnny said. "I should've gotten a sandwich like you guys told me to."

"It's your own fault, man," Jack said as he took a huge bite out of his sandwich.

Liam pursed his lips as he said, "Here," and he handed Johnny his sandwich.

Johnny's eyes lit up. "Really!?"

Liam nodded, "I'm not hungry anyways," he lied.

"Thanks, dude! You're a real lifesaver!" Johnny took a huge bite out of the sandwich.

Liam just nodded as he forced out a grin and pulled out his second Dr. Pepper from out of the bag and started to drink it. "I still got my drink left, so, whatever. No big deal."

The sandwiches were gone within seconds and Liam was left hungry. But he didn't care. He still had a Dr. Pepper left, like he said.

Johnny let out a groan as he stretched his arms up and yawned. "How long's it been anyways? Should we reapply sunscreen?"

Jack just shrugged, "I'm sure we'll be fine."

"Here," Johnny said grabbing a bottle of sun-lotion. "I'm goin' to put on some just in case." He started to reapply.

Jack just shrugged as Liam also started to reapply.

"I'll do it later," Jack said, but he never did.

"Guys, do you hear that?" asked Liam as he slowly stood up and started to reel in his fishing line.

"Hear what?" asked Jack.

"I think a trains comin'," Liam said as he slipped on his bag and continued to reel in his line.

Johnny pressed his hand against the metal tracks. "Yeah, one's comin' alright. I can feel the rumblin' in the tracks."

"Okay," Liam continued, "let's get outta its way." Liam quickly finished reeling in his line as he started to walk off of the railroad bridge and over to where everyone had left their bikes.

Johnny quickly picked up his jukebox and slipped on his backpack as he ran over to where Liam was standing.

"Jack, come on," Liam said as Jack stumbled over to them.

The train was finally in view as the three boys stood out of its way. When the train passed them a rush of wind blew everyone's hair into their eyes.

Johnny let out a sigh of relief as he said, "You never really know how hot ya're until you think that a trains wind is refreshing."

Jack chuckled with a slight smile stretched across his face. "Just be happy we aren't in Texas right now."

"Yeah," Liam chuckled, "I bet they have it real' bad durin' this time of year."

Once the train passed the three friends walked back onto the railroad bridge and cast out their lines. Johnny sat the jukebox next to him again as random songs started to play again.

After a while one in-particular song started to play called *"Hungry Like the Wolf."* Liam's eyes lit up as he suddenly jumped up on his feet and held the fishing rod up to his mouth like a microphone.

"Get down you weirdo!" Jack said chuckling a bit.

"No, you get up, *Jackio!*" yelled Johnny as he also hopped to his feet and stood next to Liam. He was also holding his fishing rod up to his mouth like a microphone. "Do you even know what song this is? You better not disrespect the wolf."

"I'm disrespectin' it."

"Come on, Jack," Liam said. "I thought you liked this song."

Jack pursed his lips as he thought. "Fine," he said as he slowly started to stand up.

The song started as the three boys started to dance and sing along with it.

"Darken the city, night is a wire! Steam in the subway, Earth is a fire! Do do do do, do do do, do do do, do do do!"

All of the boys smiled happily as they continued to sing and dance on top of the railroad bridge.

"Woman you want me, give me a sign, and catch my breathin' even closer behind! Do do do do, do do do, do do do, do do do!"

As Johnny sang he started to make weird faces at Liam and Jack who continued to sing.

"In touch with the ground, I'm on the hunt I'm after you! Smell like I sound, I'm lost in the crowd and I'm hungry like the wolf!"

The three boys continued to laugh and dance and sing as the song played. A few people on boats driving under the railroad bridge shot them strange looks as they continued to drive their boat. But they didn't care. Liam, Johnny and Jack didn't care what people thought of them so they continued to laugh, dance and sing until the song ended.

At the end of the day nobody caught any fish which hardly ever happened. They didn't mind though; they just enjoyed hanging out with each other and being able to talk.

They all packed up all of their items as the sun slowly started to lower in the sky. Each of them hopped on their bikes and headed back to their houses. The ride back was very uneventful, quiet, and, not to mention, cooler. Now that the sun wasn't out, it was a much more relaxing and cool ride.

When they got to the part in the road where it went into three different directions Liam said, "Well, see ya' guys Monday."

"Yeah," Johnny said, "see ya'."

"Bye, guys," Jack said.

The three of them all went separate directions toward their houses. Liam continued to ride his bike as his stomach rumbled beneath him. The sun was now tucked away behind the horizon as he rode by the comic shop with Gabe sitting out at the front.

"Good night, Gabe!" Liam waved as he passed him.

"Good night, Liam!" Gabe managed to yell back as he waved. As Gabe watched Liam ride away he chuckled to himself, "Nice, boy," and soon sleep fell upon him.

May 13, 1984

<u>Chapter 3</u>

The Train's Whistle

The sun slowly rose in the distant horizon illuminating all of Kingston, Oklahoma a faint pink morning shine. The air outside was dry. There was no dew on the morning grass or moisture in the air. There was hardly any grass left at all for the dew to set on because of how dried up it all was. With each step you took upon the crunchy, yellow grass it would sound as if tree branches were snapping.

C

   R

      U

         N

            C

               H!

Liam rode down the long road with Johnny and Jack beside him. It was still early in the morning and all three boys were tired.

"Why exactly are we doing this?" asked Jack as he shifted his head to look at Liam.

Liam shrugged. "My mom, she wanted us to go meet this new kid. Apparently, he just moved here yesterday and they're still moving in. She thought it would be cool if we met the new kid and maybe helped them move into their new house."

"Why?" asked Johnny. He didn't bother looking at Liam. His eyes remained straight ahead of him.

Liam shrugged again. "I told you I don't know. My mom just said that this new kid didn't really know anybody here and that he would really like it if we tried to be friends with him."

"But we don't need 'nother group member," Jack stated. "Three is the perfect number. Why do we haff'to invite someone new to the group."

Liam remained quiet. He didn't have an answer.

"Yeah," Johnny continued, "We're the three musketeers; the three amigos; the three—"

"I get it," Liam interrupted, "but my mom asked me to do this so that's watta'm gonna do. You guys can either help me or you can go do something else. Either way I'm stayin' here."

Liam pulled up into the driveway of a house. Boxes were scattered everywhere and the place looked like a dump.

"Fine," Johnny rolled his eyes as he hopped off of his bike and threw it down in the yard with the rest of the clutter. He didn't have anything better to do anyway.

All three of the boys walked up to the huge, wooden front door. Liam reached over and rang the doorbell. They could hear the *ding* from the inside of the house. Footsteps followed.

The door was suddenly opened only to reveal a woman's face. "Why, hello," the woman said in a high-pitched voice.

"Hi, uhm, I'm Liam and these are my friends," Liam continued as Jack and Johnny waved awkwardly. "I think you connected with my mom or somethin' and we're here to help you move in—"

"Yes," the woman said as she interrupted Liam. "Come on in," she opened the door wide enough for the boys to walk inside of her house. It was as much of a dump inside as it was outside. "Sam, get down here!" The mom yelled up the stairs. "The boys are here!"

"Uhm, I didn't catch your name—"

Liam was interrupted once again. "Mrs. Oglesby."

"Oh, uhm—"

"COMING!" yelled Sam as footsteps quickly pattered down the stairs from above. Sam skidded to a stop and he stood right next to his mom. Sam had brown hair and one of the biggest bowl-cuts a kid could have. He was about the same height as Jack and he was a little overweight. He had dark brown eyes and a grin was plastered onto his face.

"HI!" Sam yelled with excitement even though the boys were only standing a few feet apart. The three boys winced in pain from how loud his voice was as they quickly took a step back. "MY NAME IS SAM! MY MOM TOLD ME THAT—"

"Sam," his mom quietly interrupted, "do you remember what we talked about?" She looked down at him and smiled.

Sam nodded at the ground as if he were ashamed. "Yes."

"And what did we talk about?" His mother nagged on.

Sam remained looking down at the tile floor. His face was getting bright red and he refused to make eye contact with anyone. He took a deep breath in and then said very quickly, "Tokeepanormalvoicelevel." He said it so fast that it all came out with one mouth movement.

"What?" asked the mom. "You have to slow down if you want people to understand what you're saying."

Sam took a gulp. Liam could see and hear it as he took another deep breath in. "To keep a normal voice level."

"Very good!" the proud mom said as she focused her gaze back onto the boys. "Well, I'm sure I can handle all of this stuff," she paused, "so if you boys want you can just hang out with Sam for a while until I get finished."

"Uhhh—" Johnny was cut-off.

"Are you sure you don't need any help?" Jack asked trying to think up of some excuse for why he couldn't hang out with Sam. "I would h-hate for you to have to do all'vis work without any help."

"I'm quite sure," the mom said as she turned her back and walked over to some boxes and began to unpack.

"So, what do'ya guys wanna do?" asked Sam excitedly. He could hardly maintain his enthusiasm and he was about to jump out of his shoes from excitement. "We can go up to my room if ya'guys wanna?"

Jack and Johnny shot each other a *"why do we have to do this?"* look as Liam said, "Sure."

"Okay!" Sam replied frantically. "Follow me!" He motioned for them to follow him as he jolted up the stairs. The same *pattering* could be heard as he continued to climb. Liam quickly followed as Jack and Johnny stayed in the back.

"Why do we even have to hang out with this loser?" asked Jack as he shook his head in frustration as they walked up the stairs a little way behind Liam and Sam.

"Sam?"

"No, Liam," Jack chuckled sarcastically. "He's such a friggin' loser."

Johnny started to laugh as well, "We're all losers. Especially you, Jackio."

Johnny caught a playful punch to the arm from Jack. "That's what you get," Jack said as he lowered his arm and loosened his fist.

"Okay, okay," Johnny said as he rubbed his arm. "I guess I had that comin'."

"WHOA!" They heard Liam's enthusiastic voice echo from upstairs. "GUYS, HURRY! YOU HAVE TO COME SEE THIS!"

Jack and Johnny shot each other a quick glance before stumbling up the stairs after one another. From below it probably sounded like a stampede of animals on top of the house. Once they made it to the top of the stairs Jack and Johnny came to an immediate halt and their jaws dropped.

"Isn't it cool?" asked Liam, refusing to make eye-contact with Jack and Johnny. He had never seen anything so insane in his life.

"This is my room," Sam said as he held out his arms. Star Wars posters were hanging up on the wall in almost every corner of the room and action figures of every single character from the movies were standing beneath them. He had plastic lightsabers sitting on display of every color and a VHS of every movie was sitting next to them. He had even created a whole reenactment of the scene in Star Wars where Luke lost his arm with the tiny figurines he had. A huge Millennium Falcon hung from the ceiling above the display of characters. In the pilot's seat was Han Solo and right next to him was Chewbacca. Also, in another area of his room were comics. He had them all. Posters with Marvel logos were hung up on the wall behind his collection and they were all lined up in alphabetical order. They even had tabs in between each comic that told you what letter it was starting with. It was just like the comic shop that was near everyone's house except a little smaller. Just like the Star Wars figurines, he had Marvel figurines on display. Spiderman stood firmly on the ground while he fought against Dr. Octopus. Green Goblin was hovering slightly above them. Just like the Millennium Falcon, Green Goblin was hanging from the ceiling and had a bomb in hand and ready to throw. There were also Batman and Superman comics along with a few other DC superheroes but Sam didn't have a poster up with DC's logo like he did Marvel. Not only was the place a sick hangout but it was huge!

"This is your room?" Liam asked in awe as he ran over to the comic section and started to flip through the different types of comics he had.

"Yep," Sam folded his arms and nodded.

"Bro, this is sick," Johnny said as he ran over and picked up a lightsaber on display. "Is it okay if we play with these?"

"Sure, if you want," Sam said as he walked over to the lightsabers and picked one up. "This one is Obi-Wan's." He flung it out as a blue blade extended from the base.

"Whoa!" Johnny looked at it with eyes full of amazement. "Where's Luke's?"

"Which one?" Sam asked setting Obi-Wan's lightsaber back on the shelf where he had picked it up from. "Luke's blue or green lightsaber."

"You have them both!?"

"Yeah... d-dude?" Sam questioningly stammered as he walked over to two lightsabers standing up right next to each other. "So, what'll it be?"

"GREEN!" Jack called dibs as he ran over to Sam.

"Dang it! This is why we'll never be true friends," Johnny slapped Jack's back with the palm of his hand. "This's also why Samantha won't date ya', Jackio."

"Because I called dibs on Luke's green lightsaber before you could?" Jack folded his arms waiting for Johnny's response.

"Uhhh, YEAH! Why else do you think she's dating that friggin' idiot instead of you!?" Johnny laughed, "Well, actually, I take that back. You're both friggin' idiots."

Jack rolled his eyes as Sam asked, "Wait, who's Samantha?"

"One of Jackio's stupid crushes," Johnny said as he snatched the blue lightsaber out of Sam's hand and flipped out the blue blade. "Isn't it, Jackio?" He started to poke Jack, tauntingly, with the tip of the lightsaber.

"Wait, *one* of his stupid crushes? As in he has more than one crush?" Sam asked.

"Not that we know of," Johnny continued to poke Jack, "but he probably has like twenty."

"Have you read the new Secret Wars issue yet?" asked Liam. He continued to dig through the comics that were on the shelf.

"I've read it," Sam continued as he handed Jack Luke's green lightsaber, "but I don't own it." He walked over and sat down right next to Liam. "But to be really honest with you, all this stuff is just a side-hobby."

"So, you have something else that you like more than comics and Star Wars?" Liam started to put the comics back on the shelf in alphabetical order like they were when he came in.

"Yeah," Sam said. "I can show you if you want."

"Uhh, sure," Liam said as he stood up.

"It's in another room but I'm not sure if you'll find it as interesting as I do," Sam started to walk to a different room.

Liam followed Sam as Johnny and Jack continued to *whack* each other with lightsabers on the other side of the room.

Sam opened up a door and walked into the room. "This is my favorite room."

Liam walked inside with Sam.

Train tracks circled the whole room and movie posters of *Murder on the Orient Express* were hung on the walls.

"Even though the movie came out 1934, it's my favorite movie of all time," Sam confessed.

"So, you like... trains?" Liam asked.

"Yeah, it's pretty weird," Sam admitted.

"N-no. I know m-many people that like tr-trains," Liam stammered.

"It's fine. I know it's weird. I wanna be a conductor when I grow up," Sam stated.

"Oh."

A long pause of silence followed. The only thing that could be heard was the occasional laughter from Jack and Johnny as they continued to fight in the other room. Finally, Sam broke the silence. "I get that you like comics and Star Wars more than this stuff, but I just thought that I'd show you—ya' know?"

Liam nodded, "Yeah, I get it."

"So, does that mean that'cha have something that you like more than comics and Star Wars?" asked Sam hopefully.

"I mean, we're all into comics and Star Wars—I just happen to be more into comics," Liam paused as he looked through the doorway at Jack and Johnny who continued to fight. "As you can see these idiots are more into Star Wars."

Sam nodded as he looked a Jack and Johnny with Liam. They were definitely acting like idiots. They looked like idiots too.

"Yeah—I, uhm—I wanna be a comic writer when I grow up," Liam confessed. "I don't have a clue what these guys wanna be though," he pointed at Jack and Johnny.

"So, you like writing?" asked Sam.

"Well, kinda. Not necessarily writing as much as I just like comics in general. I think it'd be cool to create short stories or scripts, but anything to do with the comic business would be awesome."

"So, you'd be okay with just drawing pictures for a comic?" asked Sam.

"Yeah, I guess."

"Cool," Sam looked up at Liam, "I just like readin' them."

"Yeah," Liam chuckled, "I like readin' them too."

"So," Sam started to walk out of the room, "what're some of the stuff that you guys do for fun 'round here?"

"Well," Liam followed Sam out of the room as he closed the door behind him, "we could go to the beach. We went fishing yesterday but we didn't catch anything unfortunately."

Sam nodded, "So, is that all you guys do around here—fish and swim?"

"Well," Liam continued, "we also ride our bikes around town; we could explore the woods; go to the arcade; there's a buncha stuff we could do. We also go to the comic store near our houses. Just name it. Whatever you wanna do."

Sam curled his upper lip. "How 'bout we just go to the beach," he suggested.

"Sure," Liam said walking into the middle of Jack and Johnny's duel.

"I'LL GO GET MY SWIMMING TRUNKS!" Sam yelled excitedly as he leaped down the stairs.

Liam held up his hands as he stood in between Johnny and Jack. "Guys, we're gonna go to the beach with Sam. Maybe show him 'round a bit."

Jack and Johnny immediately stopped swinging their lightsabers and shot each other a quick glance. They locked eye for about three seconds before nodding at each other.

"Guys, what?" Liam asked, confused about what his friends were doing.

Without hesitation Jack and Johnny started hitting Liam with their lightsabers. Liam immediately fell to the ground and curled up into a ball and started to laugh. Johnny and Jack started to laugh too as they continued to hit Liam with their lightsabers.

"Guys, stop!" Liam chuckled as he remained in a fetal position.

"What's the magic word?" Jack asked tauntingly with a sly grin spread across his face.

"I ain't gonna say no magic word to'ya. You're the one that has a crush on someone outta your league," Liam laughed.

"What'd you say?" asked Jack as he continued to teasingly hit Liam with his green lightsaber. "I could've sworn that you just—"

"That's because I did, you idiot!" Liam interrupted as he slowly tried to regain balance and stand up on his feet again.

Johnny started laughing and instead of hitting Liam some more he switched his attack back to Jack. Soon no body was hitting Liam anymore and Jack and Johnny were hitting each other with lightsabers again.

"Guys," Liam said once he regained his balance and stood up, "did either of you learn any proper manners when you were a child?"

Neither of them answered as they both stopped hitting each other and turned back around to Liam.

"Didn't your mom ever teach you that hitting people with sticks was considered rude?" Liam asked, fully prepared to be ambushed by Jack and Johnny's lightsabers again.

"No," Johnny said plainly, "but *your* mom told me that she actually preferred being hit by my stick," Johnny smiled cleverly.

"Screw you," Liam chuckled, "I should've seen it comin'."

"HEY-OOO!" Jack replied to Johnny's comment as he raised a hand in the air.

"You're one to talk, Jackio," Johnny turned to Jack grinning even more. "You probably don't even have a stick."

"No wonder Samantha won't date you," Liam quickly added.

The grin on Jack's face immediately disappeared and Liam and Johnny burst out into laughter. Liam fell to the ground with laughter as he struggled to catch his breath as Johnny just stood there smiling, his arms crossed.

Jack shook his head with a frown spread across his face. "Idiotic," he muttered to himself as he walked over to Johnny and started to hit him with his lightsaber again.

"Bye, mom!" Sam yelled behind him as the boys walked out of the house. Sam was the only one with swim trunks on—everyone else was just going to swim in their normal clothes.

"Bye!" she quickly called back from the back of the cluttered, box-filled house. "You boys be safe!"

"We will!" Sam called back as he closed the front door. He turned back around to look at Liam, Jack, and Johnny. "I'MA GO GET MY BIKE!" He quickly yelled with excitement as he rushed to the side of his house—probably where his bike was.

Once Sam was out of sight Jack leaned in and said, "I'm not tryin' to be mean, but Sam's really weird. He's always yellin' for no reason and—" Jack was interrupted before he could finish.

"Dude," Liam continued somewhat offended, "you know he has autism, right?"

"Autism?" Johnny asked confused. "What's that?"

"It's a type of brain thing. Like, something's wrong with his brain," Liam scrunched up his eyebrows.

"Wh-what?" Jack stammered as Johnny shook his head. Neither of them knew. "Sorry, Liam. I-I didn't know."

"Yeah—uhm—neither did I," Johnny paused. "But Sam seems pretty cool—his Star Wars and comic collection is pretty dope."

Liam just squinted even more, causing his eyebrows to cover his eyes as he shook his head with disgust. "Just—ya'know—don't. Okay?"

"Liam," Jack continued, full of regret. "I'm sorr—"

"Don't," Liam repeated, interrupting Jack.

"OKAY!" Yelled Sam from the side of the house as he started to walk toward everyone else. "I FOUND MY BIKE!"

"Let's go," Liam said plainly as he hopped on his bike and started to ride off ahead of everyone else.

Sam looked over at Jack and Johnny with confusion. "Why is he so upset?"

Jack and Johnny shot each other a quick glance before looking back at Sam. Johnny just shrugged and said, "I don't know," and he sped off after Liam.

"Here," Jack continued, "let's get goin' and I'll tell you along the way." He hopped on his bike and started to pedal behind Johnny. Sam was to Jack's left as they continued down the road.

"So, why was Liam upset?" Sam asked once they caught a good pace.

"He—well—he had an uncle with down syndrome. Kinda like you with..." Jack's voice trailed off as he caught himself, not wanting to offend Sam.

"Had?" asked Sam.

Jack nodded sadly. "He died a few years ago. They were—" Jack paused, "—were really close. Like father and son close."

"Wait," Sam paused, "DOES LIAM NOT HAVE A DAD!?"

"No—no—he does. He's just never really been too close to his dad. He never really talks to Liam. Kinda just ignores him. His uncle was his main source of comfort—other than his mom," Jack said as he looked down at his shadow beneath him.

"So, what happened to his uncle?" Sam asked.

"He contracted ALS. I don't know if you know what that—"

"I know what it means," Sam confirmed as he continued to pedal beside Jack.

"Well, yeah. That's what happened," Jack sniffled some.

"So, why was Liam so upset?" Sam asked.

"We—we just—we just made a personal remark involving his uncle. We didn't do it on purpose, it's just, sometimes—"

"Stuff just slips out without you meanin' for it to," Sam nodded understandingly. "Trust me, from someone who talks a lot—and I mean A LOT—I understand." Sam took in a deep breath, "Let's go see what Johnny's up to."

Jack smiled as he nodded and they sped off toward him. Once they caught up to Johnny and caught a good pace again they started talking.

"What's up, Johnny?" asked Jack pulling up next to Johnny.

Johnny just shrugged, "Nothin'," he looked over in Liam's direction, "I just hope he doesn't act like this all day."

"He won't," Jack continued. "The last time something like *this* happened he forgot about the whole situation within ten to twenty minutes. Trust me, he has trouble stayin' mad or holdin' a grudge."

Johnny nodded, hoping Jack was right. Liam was usually always nice and high-spirited. He hated it whenever Liam was down in the dumps. "Okay," Johnny continued, "we'll just haff'to wait an' give him space and time."

"Hey," Sam butted in, "how far away is the beach again? This is actually the first time I've gone anywhere around town beside my neighborhood and house." He was already getting tired and was a little out of breath. Johnny was also starting to work up a little sweat.

"Not far. Around fifteen miles," Jack said as he continued to pedal.

"FIFTEEN MILES!?" yelled Sam, surprised by how far away the beach was. "I THOUGHT IT WOULD BE LIKE ONE OR TWO MILES! NOT FIFTEEN!"

"Don't worry," Johnny said, "it's not that bad. Plus, when we get to the beach we'll be nice an' hot an' ready to jump into the cold water. I think it makes it better."

"About forty-five minutes from our houses if we travel at this pace. Maybe around an hour if we take a few breaks," Jack stated.

"Yeah," Sam said, "I might need to take a break. I haven't ridden my bike in a really long time and I'm really outta shape."

Johnny chuckled, "Yeah, well we usually stop and take a break when we get up to the gas station. We usually just get some food and drinks and relax a lil' bit," Johnny pointed ahead of them. "But that's about twenty minutes away from here. You think you can hold out until then?"

Sam nodded, "Yeah, I'll be fine. It's just really hot outside."

"Good," Johnny said. "The hotter it is, the better it'll be when we get there."

Sam nodded in agreement.

"Oh!" Jack nearly yelled, "I forgot! Did either of you bring any money. I didn't bring any because I didn't think we was plannin' on goin' to the beach." Jack looked at Johnny and Sam with pleading eyes. "Either of you?"

"I'm sorry," Sam continued, "I forgot. I didn't even know that we were gonna be stopping by a gas station an' gettin' drinks."

"Johnny?" Pleaded Jack.

Johnny shrugged, "I didn't know 'bout it either. I mean—I—I knew 'bout the gas station, but not that we were goin' to the beach. Sorry, Jackio."

Jack rolled his eyes, "It's fine. But I gotta tell ya'—"

"What?" Johnny interrupted.

"I'm not a big fan of that new nickname that you gave me," Jack confessed.

"That's the point," Johnny smiled slyly.

Jack sighed.

"Wait, what about this nickname?" asked Sam.

"Jack's an idiot—so I make fun of him," Johnny smirked.

Jack shook his head annoyingly. "Idiot," he muttered under his breath.

"What was that, Jackio?" asked Johnny sarcastically as he pretended to lean in closer to hear what he had to say.

"I SAID—"

"Yeah," Johnny interrupted, "I heard what you said you, nimrod! I swear, for a guy with glasses you're pretty stupid."

"What're you implying?" asked Jack.

"That you're stupid."

"No, about the glasses."

"What about them?"

"ARE YOU IMPLYING THAT PEOPLE WITH GLASSES ARE SMARTER THAN NORMAL PEOPLE!?" yelled Jack.

"I *was*. But I guess that's not the case, clearly. Especially when someone like you wears them," Johnny pointed at Jack.

Jack just shook his head in disbelief as he looked over at Sam. "You see this? I'm still surprised that we've remained friends this whole time. He's always so mean to me."

"I think you're both mean to each other," Sam claimed.

"He's gotta point, Jackio," Johnny agreed.

"But you gotta admit, he's meaner to me than I am to him," Jack nodded.

"I mean," Sam paused, "I guess."

"Hah!" Jack called out.

"*Hah!*" Johnny mocked.

Jack rolled his eyes, "I'm just—"

"*I'm just—*"

"Speechless."

"*Speechless.*"

"See what I mean?' asked Jack glancing over to Sam.

"*See what I mean?*"

Jack shook his head again. "I'm just, not gonna talk."

"*I'm just, not gonna talk.*"

Sam started to laugh, "You're both *idiots*," he repeated Jack.

"HEY, GUYS!" Liam's voice came from up ahead. "COME LOOK AT THIS!"

Jack, Johnny, and Sam all shot each other a quick glance of confusion.

"GUYS! HURRY!"

Everyone quickly started to pedal toward Liam's voice, curious as to what he could be wanting to show them.

"What is it?" asked Johnny pedaling up beside Liam.

Liam didn't look at Johnny. His gaze remained fixated in front of him. Liam didn't respond, he just nodded as if saying "*Look in front of you.*"

Johnny turned his head and coasted to a stop into the gas station parking lot next to Liam. Soon Jack and Sam coasted up next to them as well. Nobody could be seen through the gas station windows and all of the lights that were usually on inside were off. A red **CLOSED** sign had been flipped around on the door. Liam quickly hopped off of his bike, throwing it to the ground, and walked up to the closed gas station. He grabbed the door handle and pulled it, but it was locked.

"That's weird—the gas station is never closed. Not even on the weekends," Jack stated as he walked up next to Liam and stood outside of the gas station, trying to peer through the glass door.

"So—I guess it doesn't matter that we all forgot money," Johnny said hopping off of his bike. "But it would be nice to relax a little. I need to catch my breath." He pulled out his inhaler and started to breathe through it as he walked over to a patch of yellow, crispy, dried grass and sat down. He wiped the sweat off of his forehead as he laid down in the grass and looked up at the sky.

"I wonder what happened," Liam said as he tried to open the gas station door again.

"So—what—no sodas?" asked Sam, somewhat disappointed.

"I guess not," Jack said turning around and walking away from the gas station.

"Hey, you don't think—" Liam stopped himself.

"What?" asked Jack.

Johnny—who was lying down—sat up and looked over at Liam. "Yeah. What?"

"You don't think ol' Chipper finally—" he didn't finish the statement. He just clicked his tongue, whistled, and drew a line across his neck.

Jack raised an eyebrow. "Ya' think?"

"Maybe," Liam said. "He was really old."

"Nah," Johnny shook his head, still sitting in the patch of dried grass.

"Why nah?" asked Jack.

"Who's Chipper?" asked Sam confused about this whole conversation.

"An ol' dog that basically lives here," Liam nodded.

"Just because, I don't think Chipper would die this early," Johnny replied to Jack.

"What do ya' mean?" asked Jack, full of confusion. "We were just talkin' yesterday about how Chipper would die any day now."

"I was just jokin'," Johnny said.

"How old was Chipper?" asked Sam.

"Ol' enough to be—" Liam whistled and drew another line across his neck again.

"Ya' don't know his actual age?" asked Sam.

Liam shrugged, "Not really."

"I bet Cap'n Cosmo's just takin' a sick day," Johnny suggested.

"I've never seen Cosmo sick," Jack pointed out.

"Who the heck is Cap'n Cosmo!?" asked Sam.

"The guy who runs this joint," Liam replied.

"Well, everyone gets sick," Johnny said.

"Yeah, I know. I've just never seen *Cosmo* sick."

"Okay, whatever," Johnny rolled his eyes.

"I hate to admit it," Jack said, "but he could be."

"So, you think he is?" Liam questioned.

"I don't really *think* anything. I'm just sayin' that it's a possibility," Jack pointed out.

"Well, it really doesn't matter," Johnny said. "All we know is that Cap'n Cosmo's gone and that's it. Chipper could be dead, but Cosmo could also just be sick. Let's just get goin'. That nice refreshin' lake water sounds better than ever right about now."

Liam shrugged. "Yeah, we should probably get goin'. It is getting' pretty hot out and we're almost there."

"At least halfway," Jack pointed out.

"Okay, then. What're we waitin' for? LET'S GO TO THE LAKE!" yelled Sam as he hopped on his bike, ready to go.

Liam smirked as he walked over and hopped on his bike too. "Okay. Let's go."

By the time everyone made it to the beach they were all drenched in sweat and ready to jump into the nice, cool, refreshing lake water. Even though it wasn't summer yet it was still raging hot. It always was in Kingston, Oklahoma. Summer always came early, and winter always came late. It was the way things worked around there. They had never thought anything of it. They had grown accustomed to the raging summers and the freezing winters. The only thing they ever thought about the summers was how grateful they were that they didn't live in Texas. It must've been twice as hot as it was in Kingston. Texas wasn't just raging hot in the summers; it was a full-on inferno of fire blazing down on the dried wastelands. That's what the kids thought anyway. Little did they know that Texas was generally no hotter than Oklahoma.

"Well, here it is," Liam said coasting up to the beach and hopping off of his bike. "Boat Ramp Beach!"

"It's 'bout friggin' time," Johnny said hopping off next to Liam and throwing his bike on the ground. Dust was thrown up into the air from Johnny's sneakers scraping against the ground and the bike. The wind blew the sand that had been kicked up into the air right into Jack and Sam's face.

Jack and Sam coughed their way over to Johnny where they threw down their bikes as well. "Come on, Johnny!" Jack coughed as he playfully punched Johnny in the arm.

"What," asked Johnny, "can't handle a little sand to the face?"

"Let's see you take a hand full of sand to the face!" Sam coughed.

"I'ma 'bout to give him a fist to the face," Jack chuckled as he took off his thick glasses and wiped the sand off of them with the end of his shirt.

Liam quickly slipped off his T-shirt and threw it down in a ball on the ground next to the bicycles that laid on top of one another. He quickly slipped off his sneakers and threw them over next to his crumpled shirt and peeled off his socks as he hopped over to the lake. He quickly threw his sweaty socks over next to his shoes and stepped into the cool water. He then dove into the lake and went underwater where he stayed for a few seconds before breaking surface again. Liam let out a sigh of relief as he laid down in the water and closed his eyes.

"HOW'S IT FEEL!?" yelled Johnny from the beach. He was also taking off his shoes and socks and was already shirtless.

"AMAZING!" Liam yelled back. "I DON'T THINK IT'S BEEN THIS HOT SINCE 1982!"

"AHHH!" Johnny sighed, "1982!"

"Whatta *B*," Jack muttered under his breath, just loud enough for Sam and Johnny to hear him.

"What happened in 1982?" asked Sam as he started to take off his shoes.

Johnny shook his head, "Trust me, just be happy that you didn't move here *that* year. It was the hottest summer that any of us have ever, and probably will ever, live to see." Johnny quickly stumbled into the lake after Liam.

"Man," Jack said, "I love Boat Ramp Beach. It's a shame we don't visit it more."

"Why don't you?" asked Sam as he walked across the hot, sandy beach toward the lake where Liam and Johnny were.

Jack shrugged as he walked alongside Sam. "I don't know. We just have so many other things that we enjoy doing more. Most of the times it's too hot, though."

"HOTTER THAN THIS!?" yelled Sam, surprised.

"We haven't even scraped the surface," Jack chuckled as he jumped into the water and let out a sigh of relief.

Hours went by as the kids played in the lake. Strangely enough nobody else was there and the kids were all alone.

"Hey, hey," Jack continued, "watch this." He quickly dove under water. There was no sign of him for a couple of seconds. Everyone got quiet. Finally, Jack's feet emerged from the water and his legs were straight up in the air.

"IS HE DOIN' A HAN' STAN'!?" Sam laughed as he held his stomach.

Johnny rolled his eyes as he walked over to Jack and looked over at Sam and Liam. "He makes it too easy for me." He grabbed one of Jack's legs and pushed it over causing him to fall down.

Liam started to chuckle.

Jack resurfaced as he took in a deep breath of air and glared at Johnny. "You're a little—"

"It's not my fault," Johnny confessed. "You just make it way too easy."

Jack swiped the wet, black hair out of his eyes as he filled his mouth with dirty lake water. He quickly spit it out onto Johnny in a straight line.

"Oh, come on, Jack. That's disgusting," Liam shook his head.

Jack shrugged uncaringly.

"Hey, Sam," Liam continued, "Isn't that disgusting?"

Sam didn't respond. Sam was standing waist deep in the water as he looked over at the railroad bridge as the train crossed over it.

"Hey, Sam?" asked Liam. "You okay?"

Everyone got quiet as they looked at Sam.

"Do you ever just wonder where they're goin'?" asked Sam.

Jack and Johnny shot a quick glance at each other before Johnny tackled Jack into the water.

"What the f—" Jack yelled out before his body became submerged in water.

"Whatta ya' mean?" asked Liam as he stepped closer to Sam who refused to take his focus off of the moving train. Jack and Johnny continued to fight each other in the background.

The train whistle blew. "I dunno. I just—I always thought that maybe there was somethin' more to a train than just cartin' stuff 'round. Ya' know?" Sam looked at the train with awe.

"I mean—" Liam was interrupted.

"I know it sounds stupid, but don't ya' ever just wonder where—if you got on the train—the train would take you?"

"I mean—" Liam repeated.

"Nevermind," Sam quickly said. "It's stupid. Just forget 'bout it." Sam turned around and looked at Liam. "My mom's gonna be wondering where I'm at soon. We should probably start headin' back." Sam walked out of the water and onto the beach where he started to put his clothes back on.

Liam nodded as he got Johnny and Jack and they all followed Sam out of the lake. They slipped their clothes back on and started to bike their way home.

The ride was quiet as usual. Everyone was tired and ready to get home.

It took longer to get back to their houses than it took to get there. They were exhausted from the day's activities. Sam eventually split away from the group and headed toward his house as everyone said "bye". One by one everybody split away from the group until it was just Liam left. He was tired but instead of going home he pulled up to the comic shop.

Gabe was sitting out front as usual resting his tired body on the back wall. He looked half asleep.

Liam hopped off of his bike and walked over to Gabe and sat down next to him. The sun was slowly setting and it was starting to get a little chilly outside. The comic shop had already closed but the lights were still on and Glenn was still inside. He practically lived in the comic shop.

Gabe, to Liam's right, started to shiver in his sleep even though he had a jacket around him. That was the thing about Kingston. It was dreadfully hot during the day, and painfully cold in the nights.

Liam stood up and walked into the comic shop. The bell rung above the door as Glenn stood behind the counter stacking comics.

"Hey, Liam. Sorry, we're closed," Glenn said glancing up at Liam who walked up to the front counter. "And shouldn't you be home this time of night?"

"Ahh," Liam swatted the air with his hand, "don't sweat it. It'll be fine."

Glenn nodded. "'Kay. So, what can I do for ya'?"

Liam shrugged, "I don't really wanna buy anything."

"Oh, yeah?"

"I was just—I wanted to ask you a question," Liam stated.

"Shoot," Glenn replied.

"And I know this is kinda outta the blue but," Liam paused as he tapped his fingers on the desk, "do you know who Gabe is?"

"You mean that guy outside?" asked Glenn.

"Yeah."

"Yeah. I know him. We've talked several times," Glenn said.

"Well, he seems pretty cold. Do you have a blanket or something I could bring out to him?" Liam asked. "I mean, you do practically live here."

Glenn smiled sadly and something sparkled in his eyes as he said, "Sure," and headed to the back of the comic shop that Liam had visited for the first time earlier that week. A few minutes passed before Glenn came back out with a blanket. "Will this do?" He held up the blanket.

Liam nodded, "Perfect."

Glenn handed it over to Liam.

"Thanks," Liam said.

"Hey, no problem," Glenn said. The sad look still lingered in his eyes from before. Liam smiled as he turned around and started to walk out of the store. He was halfway through the door when Glenn said, "Hey, Liam," Liam turned to face Glenn, "if anything ever happens or if you need help or a place to stay or anythin', you come on by, 'kay?"

Liam nodded once as he turned and walked out of the comic store. Glenn watched as Liam quickly laid the blanket on top of Gabe and hopped on his bike and rode away.

Glenn turned the lights off and walked to the back room.

As he closed the door behind him and got undressed and put on his pajamas he laid down in a makeshift mattress that he had made from piling blankets on top of one another. He slowly pulled a blanket up on top of him as he closed his eyes, squeezing out two tears that rolled down his rosy cheeks.

May 14, 1984

Chapter 4

Slap-Jack

"HEY, LIAM!" hollered Gabe as Liam rode his bike past the comic shop and to school. One more month; just one more month until summer. Gabe held up the blanket that Liam had covered him up with the night before. "THANKS FOR THE BLANKET!"

"THANK GLENN. IT'S HIS BLANKET!" Liam replied as he continued to ride his bike toward his school.

The pink morning sun started to rise in the distant horizon. The wind blew through his dirty blonde hair as a slight chill ran up his spine. A faint dew rested on the dry, yellow grass as Liam heard someone call his name. He immediately turned his head to his right where the voice had come from.

Johnny pedaled up next to Liam as he said, "Hey."

"What're you doin' up so early? Ya' usually don't ev'n get to school until the bell rings," Liam replied as he slowed down his pace to match Johnny's speed.

Johnny shrugged, "I dunno. Ya' always say how much ya' like to get a head start on the day. Guess I just thought that I might try'n take a piece of advice from ya'."

"Well that's a first," Liam smirked. "Are ya' sure that's it? I can't think of any other time that you took some advice from me without me forcin' you to do it."

"Well—" Johnny paused, "—I did wake up really early an' I couldn't go back to sleep. That might have somethin' else to do with it."

Liam rolled his eyes. "Yeah! You're talkin' 'bout yourself like you take advice from me. I see how it is. I guess I better just go an' make sure to take some advice from you, now don't I? YEAH RIGHT!" Liam scoffed, "you're gonna be the last person I take advice from."

"Even before Jack?" asked Johnny.

Liam nodded, "That's what I said."

"Sorry," Johnny said scratching at the inside of his ear with his pinky. "It's kinda hard to tell when you have a voice like that."

Liam rolled his eyes. "I'm startin' to see why Jack hates ya' so much."

"Aww," Johnny paused, "Jackio doesn't hate me. He loves me—almost as much as he loves Samantha Beasley."

Liam smirked as he chuckled to himself. "Ya' know, there will be a day when me and Jack find out who you have a crush on."

"I've already told you who it is," Johnny replied as he raised an eyebrow.

"You have? Who?"

"Your mom."

"SHUT UP, MAN!" Liam burst out into laughter. "Ya' know one of these days my mom's gonna hear you say somethin' like that and she's not gonna let me hang out with ya' anymore."

Johnny held up his hand with his fingers crossed. "We can all hope."

Liam started to laugh again. "No—but seriously—my mom will hear you one of these days and she'll think you're some sort of creep. She probably won't even know that you're jokin' and just think that you're some purvey middle school boy that likes to hit on older women."

Johnny looked at Liam and smiled. "Well, she's not wrong." He made his eyebrows dance above his eyes.

"OH MY GOD, DUDE! YOU ARE ACTUALLY THE WEIRDEST PERSON I KNOW!" Liam yelled.

"That's the mission," Johnny snapped his fingers and pointed at Liam.

"Whatever," Liam continued, "I don't even know why I hang out with you. All you ever do is put weird thoughts into my head that I can never seem to get out!"

"Like what? Me and your mom doin' it?" asked Johnny. His eyebrows were still dancing above his eyes.

"I will actually stop, go back home, and tell my parents that I need to take a sick day," Liam threatened.

"But that would be lying," Johnny mocked.

"No, it wouldn't. I'm actually starting to feel nauseous from talkin' to you."

"That's th—"

"I swear to god, Johnny, if you say 'that's the mission' then I'm gonna friggin' kill myself!" Liam stated.

Johnny started to laugh. "THAT'S THE MISSION!"

"That's it. I guess I have to kill myself," Liam said. "I did swear after all."

Johnny started laughing. "Nah, dude."

"But I swore, and I'd never lie," Liam mocked.

Johnny started to laugh some more until eventually the wind carried it away. "Hey, Liam?"

"Yeah?"

"All jokin' put aside—" Johnny paused.

"What?" Liam nagged on.

"Ah, never mind. Forget it." Johnny looked down at the pavement beneath him.

"No!" Liam pleaded. "What? Tell me!"

"You'll just laugh."

"Dude, I won't."

"Swear?"

"I swear," Liam said. "Although I guess I also swore to kill myself earlier but whatever."

"I don't know, dude."

"Johnny, you can tell me anything," Liam continued. "And I know that it's gonna be kinda hard for you with your body changing an' stuff. Well, this is the age that it starts to happen and if there is anything you want to talk with me about I will always be here for you."

Johnny rolled his eyes. "Forget it."

"Okay, dude. I'm sorry. What is it?" Liam apologized.

"Okay, well, all jokin' put aside—" Johnny paused.

"JOHNNY, FOR THE LOVE OF GOD WOULD YOU JUST TELL ME WHAT IS WRONG!?" Liam yelled somewhat annoyed.

"Okay, okay. Here it is—" Johnny sucked in a deep breath, "—I have been cheatin' on your mom with Jack's mom." He let out a sigh of relief. "Man, that feels good to get off my chest."

"You're an idiot," Liam said plainly as he started to speed off toward the school ahead of Johnny.

"Liam! Liam, wait up!" Johnny yelled, half laughing as he started to pedal after Liam. "I was just jokin'!"

"YOU'RE AN IDIOT!" Liam yelled from up ahead.

"OH, WAIT, NEVERMIND! I WASN'T JOKIN'! AND GUESS WHAT?" Johnny yelled.

"I DON'T WANNA HEAR IT!" Liam said as he parked his bike in a bike rack behind his school as he covered his ears.

Johnny started laughing as he pulled up next to Liam and parked his bike in the slot next to Liam's bike. "Fine," he began to laugh.

"Again, you are actually the weirdest person I know," Liam confirmed as he walked into the school building with Johnny.

"I know, but it's pretty fun to be weird," Johnny shrugged. "It's like, I can do whatever I want an' people just expect it from me now."

"So, if you were to yell somethin' out in Frizzle's class you wouldn't get in trouble at all?" asked Liam.

"Well, I guess it depends," Johnny said rubbing his chin.

"Okay, give me an example," Liam said.

"I dunno. You give me an example and I'll tell you if it'll be okay," Johnny said.

"Okay, what about 'your mom'?" asked Liam as he struggled to maintain his laughter.

"Well, it's not really bad unless it's used in the right context. It really just depends," Johnny stated as he continued to rub his imaginary beard.

"What about 'that's what she said'?"

"Same thing as 'your mom'," Johnny stated.

"Okay, I have an idea," Liam confirmed as he pointed at Johnny.

"What is it?"

"Anytime I sneeze you have to say 'your mom' and any time I cough you have to say 'that's what she said'," Liam said.

"Why?"

"It'd be fun!" Liam smiled.

Johnny shook his head. "Only if there's a reward."

"Hmm," Liam thought. "Okay, we can turn this into a competition. Loser has to buy the winner a comic of their choice."

Johnny nodded, "Okay. I'm in. How does the competition work exactly?"

"Okay, well, if I tell you to say 'your mom' or 'that's what she said' and you refuse I win," Liam nodded.

"How do I win?" Johnny asked.

"Well, if you say 'that's what she said' and 'your mom' every single time I tell you to you win," Liam confirmed.

Johnny nodded. "Sounds easy enough."

"Game on," Liam cracked a smile as they shook hands.

After a few minutes the bell rung as Jack walked into the school where Liam and Johnny were waiting. Jack walked up to Johnny and Liam who continued to talk.

"Hey guys," Jack said as he stood next to the two boys who chattered away.

"Oh, hey Jack," Liam said without looking at him.

"Hey, Jackio," Johnny continued as he turned to face Jack. "Would you like to—HOLY SH—"

"I know; I know," Jack nodded.

"WHAT HAPPENED TO YOUR FACE!?"

Liam turned to look at Jack to see what all of the commotion was about. "Dude—what happened?" Liam started to chuckle.

"I guess that this is payback for not wearing any sunscreen yesterday or Saturday," Jack shrugged. He was red—tomato red.

"Dude, does it hurt?" asked Liam pointing at Jack's face.

Jack nodded. "A little, and it's not just my face." Jack pulled up his yellow striped shirt only to reveal his stomach as red as his face. "It's everywhere. My legs are burnt to. That's why I'm wearing long pants—so no one will see how burnt I am—and trust me, these pants hurt. The material that they're made out of hurts my legs whenever I walk."

"So, you're wearing long pants so no one will see how burnt you really are?" asked Liam as he tried to contain his laughter.

"More like so Samantha Beasley won't know how burnt he is," said Johnny. "And trust me, Jackio, it's a little too late for that. I mean just look at that face! Ain't nobody gonna want to date a tomato like you, especially your girlfriend."

"DUDE, STOP!" Jack said as he held a finger up to his mouth. "You remember what happened the last time people heard I had a crush on Samantha, don't you?"

"Oh please," Johnny rolled his eyes. "For the last time, they just wanted an excuse to be douches. It's not my fault that they decided to use your stupid crush to justify chasing us into the woods and nearly beating the crap outta us! Besides, everyone knew you had a crush on her even before I said it. You made it pretty obvious to be fair."

"To be fair I just think that your sayin' that so we'll forgive you for something you did. It was your fault—again, *just bein' fair*," Jack said pointing a finger at Johnny.

"Whatever the problem is it's over," Liam continued, "and I have to get to class. See ya' guys later!" Liam said as he slapped Jack's back and ran off to first period.

"MOTHER—" Jack clenched his fists in pain and ground his teeth.

"Well, yeah. I better go also. See ya'!" Johnny said as he quickly slapped Jack's back just like Liam had done and ran off to his first class.

"YOU'RE A DOUCHE!" yelled Jack after Johnny.

"AND YOU'RE *IDIOTIC!*" replied Johnny as he continued to take off down the hallway as he mocked Jack.

Once Liam made it to history class he sat down in his usual seat and got ready for class to start. As usual Mr. White came in—his afro looking extra puffy—as he stood in front of the class and pulled out a textbook. He quickly flipped to a certain page and left it on his desk.

The bell soon rang and *almost* everyone was in class on time. Mr. White looked around the class to see one seat empty. Not soon after, Douglas flung himself into the classroom and sat down at his seat in the back of the room within five seconds.

"Ah—Douglas—late again I see," Mr. White said tapping his pencil on his desk. "One more of those and that'll be a detention."

"Uhh—y-yes—yes sir," Douglas stammered as he quickly unpacked his items and flung them on his desk.

"Thank you, Douglas, now may we proceed?" asked Mr. White.

Douglas just quickly nodded.

"Well, anyway, we have a new student joining us today!" He pointed at the doorway where Sam walked in. "Can everyone give him a big friendly welcome?" Everyone started to clap. "What's your name?" asked Mr. White.

"M-my name is Sam Oglesby and I—" Sam paused as his eyes came across Liam. "OH, HI LIAM!" Sam waved gleefully.

Liam looked up and waved slowly.

"Well, uhm, where was I. OH YEAH! My name is Sam Oglesby and I already met Liam as you can tell. I—uhm—like Star Wars and comics and—" Sam paused, "—WELL, THAT'S BASICALLY IT!"

"Well, hello Sam!" Mr. White clasped his hands together. "You'll be sitting right behind Liam."

"SWEET!" Sam quickly ran over behind Liam and slammed his stuff down on his desk. "Hey, dude," Sam whispered loudly, "what's up? Isn't this awesome! I can't believe we get to sit next to each other!"

Liam turned around and nodded. "Yeah, but when Mr. White starts talkin' be quiet so I can hear, okay?"

"Will do!" Sam said as he held a thumb up. "Oh, dude!? Did you see Jack? He's super red!"

Liam started to chuckle, "Yeah, I saw him earlier today. When did you see him?"

"When I was comin' to this class I saw him walkin' down the hall. It was hilarious! He was—like—mumblin' stuff to himself," Sam started to chuckle as he continued on. "He was sayin' stuff like how you and Johnny slapped his back. A buncha' bad stuff along with it. I even think he used your name—Liam—and another word I refuse to say."

"What was it?" Liam asked curiously.

"A bunch of stuff!"

"Hey, Liam," came Carol's voice as she sat a little way ahead of Liam and to the right. "Thanks for the comic. It was really good."

"Oh, y-yeah. No p-problem," Liam stammered quickly. "I just r-read it at one of my f-friend's house." He quickly sucked in a deep breath of air.

"Niiiice," Sam whispered to Liam sarcastically.

"Shut up!" Liam turned around and jabbed Sam in the shoulder.

"Okay, okay," Sam laughed. "But I have an idea!"

"Yeah?" asked Liam.

"We can make a game outta this," Sam said. "Let's see who can slap Jack the most out of today. Whoever does wins!"

Liam raised an eyebrow. "How are we gonna keep score?"

"Honor system," Sam continued. "No lying! We have to tell the truth. And the time you slapped Jack this mornin' doesn't count."

"Okay," Liam continued. "What does the winner get? What's the prize?"

Sam shrugged, "I dunno. What 'bout you?"

Liam thought for a couple seconds. "How about the loser has to buy the winner a soda the next time we go down to the beach?"

"Okay," Sam nodded. "Starting now!"

Liam nodded as he turned and faced the front and muttered to himself, "Two bets in one day; this could either turn out really good or really bad for me."

"Okay!" Mr. White continued, "Let's get started!"

Once the bell rang Liam headed to second period. He was a little nervous but also excited about the bet he made with Johnny.

"Hey, Liam," Jack walked up beside him. "What's up?"

"Nothin'," Liam said as he slapped Jack's back, careful not to make it too obvious he was trying to hurt him.

"AH!" Jack quickly yelled as he shook Liam's hand off his shoulder.

"Oh! Sorry, Jack. I forgot you had a sunburn," Liam lied. In his mind he counted one.

Jack rolled his eyes. "Let's just get to Frizzle's class on time. If there's one class I don't wanna be late for it's that one."

Liam nodded as he and Jack began to pick up the pace a little bit. They both entered class right as the bell rang and quickly sat down in their seats. Liam looked at Johnny who was already sitting down and was obviously nervous about the bet. His face was burrowed down in his hands and his face was already red.

"Hey, Johnny," Liam smiled as he sat down next to him. "How's it goin'?" He quickly started to pull out some of his textbooks from his bag and set them down on his desk.

Johnny rolled his eyes as he gave a sarcastic thumbs up.

"You're not nervous, are you?" Liam asked. "Now why on earth would you be nervous? Frizzle's class is always your favorite! Not to mention super fun!"

"Okay everyone," Mr. Phisel raised his hands in the air, "let's get started!"

Right as Mr. Phisel said that a wave of joy swept over Liam as a grin spread across his face. In some ways he felt bad for Johnny, that he had even agreed to this bet in the first place. There was no way that he would be able to say what Liam told him to every time. Liam held in his laughter as he tried to do a convincing cough.

Johnny winced as he quietly let out, "That's what she said."

"What was that Johnny? I'm afraid you'll have to speak up. I'm not as young as I used to be I'm afraid," Mr. Phisel smiled.

"THAT'S WHAT SHE SAID!" He said it louder this time so the whole class could hear him. A few kids in the back started to laugh as Mr. Phisel raised an eyebrow.

"D-did you just say 'that's what she said'?" he asked surprised.

"Yes," Johnny replied. "I'm sorry?"

Liam burrowed his face down into his hands cringing just at the thought of being in Johnny's shoes at that moment. Liam silently continued to laugh as Mr. Phisel walked back over to his desk. Jack was also laughing as he looked over at Johnny and asked, "What was that?"

Johnny just shook his head and gave Jack no reply.

"And what exactly does that mean, Johnny?" Mr. Phisel asked.

"I-it's very hard to explain," Johnny continued, "and I would hate to disrupt your class any more than I already have."

"Okay then," Mr. Phisel continued, "I'm just gonna ignore all of that and continue with my class if you wouldn't mind."

Johnny shook his head.

"Thank you," Mr. Phisel said as he continued to teach his class. Johnny was definitely regretting the bet he had made with Liam but he wasn't going to back down. The least he could do was put up a good fight. "So—uhm—where was I? I seem to have lost my train of thought in the midst of things.

"Johnny, do you remember where I was? I mean, you *were* the one that disrupted my class and I would sure hate to find out that you weren't following along or participating as well."

"All I heard you say was 'Let's get started' and then—" Johnny paused.

"And then what, Johnny?" asked Mr. Phisel.

"And then I made an inappropriate remark. I'm sorry," Johnny stated. He was ashamed.

"I forgive you; just don't let it happen again," Fizzle shot Johnny a cold glance as he walked back to his podium at the front of the class.

Liam started to snicker as he continued to hold in his laughter. Johnny's face turned bright red and he dug his head into his palms as embarrassment filled him head to toe. That's not why Liam was snickering or trying to contain his laughter, though. The real reason Liam was finding it so hard to maintain himself was because before class he had come in and told Mr. Phisel about everything that was about to go down. He told him about the bet, how Johnny wouldn't think anyone would care, and how the winner got a comic of his choice. Mr. Phisel had laughed at the bet and had made a deal with Liam that he would purposely be extra hard on Johnny. Liam was willing to give something in exchange to him but Mr. Phisel ultimately refused saying that getting to see Johnny that embarrassed in class was payment enough.

As Mr. Phisel walked back to his podium he shot Liam a glance and quickly winked. Liam replied with a subtle nod of the head.

"We finished our unit of the weight of gasses last week," Mr. Frizzle said once he stood up in front of his podium, "so this week can anybody guess what we're doing?"

Liam sucked in a deep breath of air debating on whether Mr. Phisel had set this up intentionally or it was just pure luck. Liam let out an obviously fake sneeze as Johnny pursed his lips and just shook his head with embarrassment.

Johnny raised his hand to answer the question praying to God that he wouldn't be called on.

"Johnny!" Mr. Phisel let out excitedly. "What are you thinking? What're we doing?"

"Y-your m-mom," Johnny whispered.

"What? You're gonna have to speak up, Johnny," Mr. Phisel said.

"Your mom," he said louder this time. Barely loud enough for the whole class to hear him. More people began to giggle and snicker in the back of the room as Mr. Phisel crossed his arms.

"Johnny, I don't appreciate the way you're acting today. One more outburst like that and I'm gonna have to punish you. Understand?"

Liam seeing an opportunity to hopefully defeat Johnny let out a quick—obviously fake—cough. As it came out Liam knew that it was game over. Johnny would never risk getting a detention over a stupid bet. His dad would never let him hear the end of it.

Johnny just shook his head in defeat as he said, "Yessir."

"Thank you, Johnny," Mr. Phisel replied as he continued to teach.

Liam leaned over to Johnny and whispered, "Nice try. I'm thinkin' X-Men issue 181. It came out the first day of May and I haven't had a chance to get it yet." He playfully jabbed Johnny with his fist as he continued. "I'll be expectin' that comic by the end of this week."

"ONE WEEK!?" Johnny whispered loudly. "I have school this whole week."

"No dip, Sherlock. The weekend!"

"Nah, man. My dad said he needed me to help him with the house this weekend," Johnny stated.

"Ah—pipe busted again?" Liam asked.

"I wish," Johnny shook his head. "Some racoons came up in our yard one night and dug through our trash. It was everywhere! My dad said that he's gonna teach me a lesson about bein' a man or somethin'. Prob'ly gonna make me kill it."

"Seriously? Does he know what happened the last time you saw roadkill?" Liam asked.

"NO," Johnny quickly said a little too loudly. "Let's keep it that way to. If he somehow finds out that I puked my guts out just from the site of a dead animal I'll never hear the end of it."

"Well, he's gonna find out one way or another," Liam stated.

"What'ya mean?"

"Well you couldn't even handle *seein'* a dead animal. How do you expect to be able to kill one?" Liam asked.

Johnny shrugged. "I'll haff'to think of somethin'."

"Okay," Liam said, "just 'cause I feel bad for you I'm gonna give ya' two weeks. But if I don't get it by the end of next week ya' owe double. Deal?"

"Deal," Johnny confirmed as he and Liam shook hands.

"Dude, what was up with Johnny?" Jack asked as he walked up to Liam after science class.

Liam shrugged and said, "I'm not sure," as he pat Jack's back just hard enough to make him wince. "Oh, sorry. I forgot about the sun-burn."

Jack nodded and rolled his eyes as he said, "Sure."

Liam just laughed and walked away as Sam approached Jack.

"Hey, Jack," Sam said. "Uhm, I have a question."

"Okay," Jack said somewhat skeptical, "what type of question?"

"What's up with Liam and Carol?"

Jack burst out in laughter, "You *already* know about it!?"

"I mean, yeah, it's pretty obvious Liam likes her," Sam said. "I mean who else would give a comic to random girl and then just start stuttering whenever she talks to you?"

"Oh my God, this is actually hilarious. If it's really that obvious then everyone at the school must know it. This is too good to pass up. Where's Johnny, I gotta tell him about this."

"So, he does, right?"

"Does what?"

"Have it bad for Carol?"

"Yeah, dude! Of course! You said it yourself didn't ya'!?"

"I guess so," Sam said still confused.

Johnny walked up to Jack and Sam, his face still burning with embarrassment from science class.

"Dude!" Jack slapped Johnny's chest with the back of his hand, "What was that in science?"

"I don't wanna talk about it."

"Okay, well get this. Sam just came up to me and asked what was up with Liam and Carol. He said it's obvious that Liam likes her," Jack said.

"Serious?" asked Johnny.

"Yeah!"

"So, I guess it's kinda like you likin' Samantha?" Johnny asked.

"Dude, shut up!"

"Calm down, Jackio," Johnny said.

Jack rolled his eyes as he murmured, "Idiot."

Johnny started to laugh, "It'll never happen." He burst out in laughter and began tearing up.

Jack just sighed.

"Well, I got what I wanted," Sam said as he slapped Jack on the back and ran away.

Once lunch started Ricky and Will sat down. Will quickly spotted Liam, Jack and Johnny sitting with Sam.

"Hey, hey, hey," Will quickly grabbed Ricky's attention.

"Huh?" Ricky asked with a mouth full of mashed-potatoes.

Ricky pointed at everyone. "Look who the retard decided to sit with."

Ricky looked over and saw Sam sitting with Liam, Jack and Johnny. Ricky quickly swallowed his food and ignored Will. He just continued to eat.

"Like, I knew he was jacked up in the head quite a bit but for anyone, even for a retard, to sit with those guys is an all-time low. One thing's for sure— retards are attracted to other retards, as you can see." Will shook his head and began to chuckle. "Like, serious—"

"Hey, will you give it a rest already?" Ricky asked. "He can't help it."

Will stopped laughing. Then started to smile. "What? Somethin' wrong? Did I just find a soft spot?"

"Dude, stop."

"I would've understood anything else bein' a soft spot but I never woulda guessed it bein' a retard. Ya' know, you could have some of that up in yer head too. Heck, what'd I say? Retards are attracted to other retards."

"I said give it a rest," Ricky commanded.

"Or what? What? What'll you do?" Will was leaning over the table and only a few inches away from Ricky's face by now. "Oh, Ricky Jason. Big boy Ricky tryin' to stick up for the lil' guy. This is a new side of him. One that I've never seen before. Tell me, what is it? Why do'ya care so much about that idiot?"

Ricky remained silent.

"Somethin' at home? Ain't that right?"

"Screw you piece of—"

"I would not finish that sentence if I were you," Will glared down Ricky. "Now, here's what's gonna happen. You're gonna tell me exactly what's goin' on that makes you care about that retard and then you're gonna apologize to me."

"For what?"

Will licked his lips. "For bein' one yourself."

"SCREW YOU!" Ricky yelled as he quickly stood up and walked away.

As Ricky walked away Will smiled. He leaned over to the kid next to him and whispered something. "I think I found a soft spot."

The rest of the day consisted of Jack getting slapped over and over again on the back until he was afraid to go anywhere. He was starting to become skeptical of Liam and Sam so he tried to stay as far away from them as possible, but that didn't work. By the end of the day Jack was just ready to get home and sit somewhere in peace. So, when the final bell rung he rushed to his locker and ran all the way home.

Liam and Sam watched him as he took off down the street and toward his house.

"Is it bad that I don't even feel sorry for him?" Sam asked.

"Same," Liam said as they both burst out in laughter.

As Jack ran down the street he heard them laughing so he turned around and yelled back to them. "YOU GUYS ARE IDIOTIC!" and then he began to run toward his house again.

Liam and Sam began to laugh harder until Jack was out of sight.

"Okay," Liam continued, "how many slaps did you get?"

"What!? I ain't sayin' mine first. You'll probably just one-up me," Sam said.

"Dude, honor system. Remember?"

Sam shrugged, "We'll say it at the same time."

"Ya' know, the fact that you don't trust me is makin' me feel bad," Liam said.

"Aw, shut up. Same time, on three." Jack paused and then began to count. "One, two, three!"

"19!" Sam yelled out.

"22"! Liam said at the same time as Sam.

"Son of a—" Sam slapped his leg in disappointment. "I guess I owe ya' a soda the next time we stop by Cap'n Cosmo's station."

"I guess ya' do."

"Lemme guess. Dr. Pepper?" Sam asked.

"Ya' know, I have only known you for like two days, and you already know me too well," Liam said as he hopped on his bike.

Sam started to chuckle to himself. "Well, I'll see ya' later," as he also hopped on his bike.

"Yep, see ya'," Liam said as he rode his bike off in the distance and smiled at the thought of him being able to drink a Dr. Pepper while reading the X-Men comic.

May 15, 1984

Chapter 5

Different Colors

R

    I

       N

         G!

The bell that signaled the beginning of school rang. Summer break sounded better than ever right at that moment. The kids were dying to get out of school and actually do something they enjoyed. The year was dragging on.

The whole day went by extremely slow. The boys' classes were boring and long, and the seconds dragged by like minutes.

They weren't given any homework, thankfully, in any of their classes except English. As the boys walked into English, their teacher greeted them. They read essays and talked about the symbolism behind certain parts of the essay. They looked at figurative language and literary terms that would 'make them better writers' according to their teacher.

The class was boring, but eventually it ended. The teacher handed out two sheets of paper to each person before they left.

"This is your homework for tonight," she stated. "I expect this to be done by tomorrow. If you paid attention in class it shouldn't be too hard."

The boys, one by one, grabbed two sheets of paper and went home.

As they exited the school building a huge heat-wave came over the boys causing them to feel exhausted without even doing anything.

"Does any of this make any sense to you guys?" Johnny asked holding up the sheet of homework in his hand. "All this symbolism crap?"

"I haven't even taken a look at it to be honest," Liam admitted.

"Well, the essay makes no sense," Johnny stated as he shoved the paper into his bag crumpling it up.

"You already read it?" Jack asked.

Johnny shrugged, "I looked over it quickly. As far as I can tell it makes absolutely no sense, whatsoever."

"Hey, guys!" Sam ran up behind the three boys from out of the school.

"Oh, hey Sam," Liam welcomed.

"Did you guys get this homework?" Sam asked as he held up the essay.

"Yeah, it makes absolutely no sense," Johnny stated. "But, we're all gonna go to my house to finish it together if you'd like to come along," Johnny invited Sam.

"No," Sam stated, "That doesn't sound like much fun."

"It's homework," Liam responded. "It's not supposed to fun. Maybe you could help us out a little?" Liam asked.

"Hmm," Sam thought, "I guess so."

Everyone hopped on their bikes, including Sam, as they all began to ride towards Johnny's house. The hot summer sun was directly overhead, and there was absolutely no breeze outside. It was terribly dry.

"Jesus," Sam wiped the sweat off his head. "It's much hotter here than it was in Michigan."

"I didn't know you moved here from Michigan," Liam stated.

"Yeah. At least there, springtime actually feels like springtime. Down here it feels like summer almost year-round."

"So, you're not enjoying the heat too much?" Jack asked.

"The heat sucks," Sam chuckled.

"Tell me about it," Johnny agreed.

"Well, I don't know. The heat's nice whenever we feel like goin' swimming," Jack pointed out.

"I guess so," Johnny shrugged.

"But I'd much rather have it be colder outside and deal with not swimming," Liam gave his opinion.

"Yeah," Johnny replied. "I'm with Liam on this one."

"I guess it does start to feel unbearable at times," Jack suggested.

"But about this essay," Sam continued, "does it make sense to you guys? I mean, I've already heard what Johnny has to say about it, but what about you, Liam and Jack?"

They both shook their heads. "I mean, I haven't read over it," Liam admitted. "I think Johnny's the only one that's at least look at it a bit."

"Same," Jack said.

"Yeah, but I haven't actually *read* it," Johnny admitted.

"Why can't we just read a book in class or somethin'?" Jack asked. "Essays are boring, and most of the time they don't make any sense."

"They have to make sense to some people. Otherwise nobody would like essays like us," Sam suggested.

"I guess," Jack shrugged. "But I don't understand why they have to make it so hard to understand most of the time. I mean, why can't they just tell a story without pasting layers and layers of metaphors and similes and all the other types of figurative language on it?"

"Yeah, it would be much easier to read if they just said what they meant," Sam stated.

"But didn't our teacher say somethin' like 'Figurative language makes writing better. Figurative language is what separates good literature from bad literature. Figurative language can drastically change the mood of the story just by adding a couple of different phrases.'?" Liam asked.

"Did she actually say that? And if so how did you remember exactly what she said?" asked Johnny, somewhat surprised.

Liam shrugged. "I added on a lot of crap. I'm pretty sure the only thing she said was 'Figurative language is good.' And then she just handed out this homework, and that was that."

The boys skidded to a stop in front of Johnny's house. They all hopped off of their bikes, throwing them to the ground as they walked up to the front door. Johnny pulled out a key from his backpack and quickly jiggled it around before the door opened.

Johnny's mom was sitting in the living room, staring at the television screen. His dad was nowhere in sight.

"Hey, mom," Johnny continued. "Where's dad?" Johnny shut the door behind them.

S

L

A

M!

The mom shrugged.

"Uhm, well, okay. Me and my friends are gonna go to my room and finish our homework," Johnny stated.

"Okay," his mom replied plainly. As she said this she closed her eyes and a single tear slid down her face.

Johnny looked back at his friends slowly. "You all can go ahead and go to my room. I'll be right there," he whispered, careful to make sure his mom didn't hear him.

Everyone nodded and walked towards Johnny's room.

"What's wrong?" asked Sam as the boys walked down the hallway.

Jack and Liam shrugged unknowingly.

As the boys were walking towards Johnny's room, they heard sniffling coming from a room closer by. It was coming from a bedroom to their right. The door was cracked open and someone was crying inside.

Sam asked, "Should we go check it out?"

"No, it's..." Liam shook his head, not knowing how to end the sentence.

"Johnny doesn't like talking about that room," Jack stated.

"Well, why?" Sam asked.

"We don't know," Liam admitted.

"Well, then let's go check it out," Sam suggested as he gestured for them to follow him.

Liam and Jack gave each other a quick glance before hesitantly following Sam.

The three boys peered into the room through the crack.

There was a twin sized bed in the middle of the room. The covers and pillows on the bed were camo-colored. Picture frames were hanging on the walls of Johnny's dad and—they couldn't make out the second character—holding rifles. They were decked out in camo in the pictures and there was a dead animal in front of them that had been shot. Three trophies sat on a shelf above the twin-sized bed and two medals hung around them. A night-stand beside the bed had a lamp on it. Three books rested in the night-stand but no one could make out what they were. A dresser sat parallel to the bed and all the drawers were shut. Above the dresser was a mirror. Hunting magnets stuck to the mirror. One said 'Hunting IS the Game' and the other said 'My Dad is My Hero'— both of which looked very faded and old. The carpet on the ground looked so old and stained that it was basically yellow and it was more hard-floor than carpet. The camo curtains on his window were wide open. Above the window was a deer head.

Johnny's dad was sitting on the edge of the bed, holding a picture frame in his hand, and staring out of the window crying. Sobbing.

The three boys heard a few words from the living room where Johnny and his mom were talking. One of which was 'birthday'. Another one was 'hunting'.

Before the kids knew it, Johnny was behind them.

Liam, Jack, and Sam immediately looked down at their feet in embarrassment and took a step away from the bedroom.

Johnny reached over and silently closed the door.

C

    R

       E

          A

            K!

Everyone was silent as Johnny led them to his room, where they read the essay silently to themselves. It was called "How it Feels to be Colored Me" by Zora Neale Hurston.

The last thing they read to themselves was:

But in the main, I feel like a brown bag of miscellany propped against a wall. Against a wall in company with other bags, white, red and yellow. Pour out the contents, and there is discovered a jumble of small things priceless and worthless. A first-water diamond, an empty spool, bits of broken glass, lengths of string, a key to a door long since crumbled away, a rusty knife-blade, old shoes saved for a road that never was and never will be, a nail bent under the weight of things too heavy for any nail, a dried flower or two still a little fragrant. In your hand is the brown bag. On the ground before you is the jumble it held--so much like the jumble in the bags, could they be emptied, that all might be dumped in a single heap and the bags refilled without altering the content of any greatly. A bit of colored glass more or less would not matter. Perhaps that is how the Great Stuffer of Bags filled them in the first place—who knows?

-Zora Neale Hurston

    And the only thing Liam understood about the passage, as he walked home from Johnny's house, was that everyone's different.
    Everyone's life is painted a different color.

May 18, 1984

Chapter 6

Fair n' Square

R

I

N

G!

The front door of the comic shop was opened as a gust of warm, early summer air blew in and sucked the cold air out of the shop.

"Whoa, close that door!" Glenn held up his hands dramatically in defense. He was standing behind his counter by the cash register as normal. "You're drivin' away my customers!"

All four of the boys took a moment to look around the store, but nobody was inside. "What customers?" Johnny asked. "Ya' know, we're like your only customers."

"Well, I wouldn't be so sure of that," Glenn said as he gave Johnny a wink.

"Yeah! Carol comes here a lot. Ain't that right, Liam?" asked Jack as he elbowed Liam on the shoulder.

Glenn smiled and asked, "How were your weeks?"

"Well, it was pretty good for me," Liam said, "because a certain someone by the name of Johnny Taylor owes me a comic of my choice."

"Oh yeah?" Glenn asked.

"Though it pains me to admit my faults, 'tis true!" Johnny shook his fist dramatically in the air.

"And I owe Liam a soda," Sam said. "We just haven't gotten 'round to that yet. Prob'ly sometime this weekend though."

"Oh, uhm," Liam stammered as he realized that Glenn was a bit confused. "This is Sam. He's new to our school and has been hangin' out with us recently."

"Oh, well, it's always nice to see new faces 'round here. Name's Glenn. My job is to basically give you or sell you any comic your heart desires."

Sam nodded and gave him a thumbs up.

"Lemme ask you a question before you get too settled in. And don't get worried, I ask all my new customers this question every single time. I've had my fair share of weird and crazy people so don't feel too intimidated. Okay, so, have you ever read a comic before, or at least tried to read one?"

"Are ya' kiddin' me!? I LOVE COMICS!" Sam exclaimed.

"Okay... Good, good. We're off to a great start, Sam. Two comic enthusiasts just chillin' and talkin' 'bout comics. If you're really that much of a comic lover I don't think it'll matter what your favorite comic is, but I'll ask anyway. What is it?"

"Like, one specific comic or a series?" Sam asked.

"Either is fine. There are no wrong answers—unless of course you pick a crappy comic. In that case you picked the wrong answer. But again, no pressure—I've had my fair share of people who like weird comics and I'm sure the worst is yet to come. So, what is it?"

"Hmmm," Sam hesitated as he rested his right index finger on his chin. "It would probably have to be Star Wars."

"Nice choice! I personally also love Star Wars. Do you have a specific issue ya' like more than the others?"

"Not really."

"No, hmm? Just like the series all together?" Glenn asked.

Sam nodded.

"Well, feel free to take some time to look 'round. 'Splore a bit and ask me any questions you want," Glenn said.

"What's in the back room?" Johnny asked.

"Not you, ya' idiot. I mean Sam."

"What's in the back room?" asked Jack.

Glenn rolled his eyes. "Did ya' not just hear what I told your friend?" he asked pointing to Johnny. "I was askin' Sam!"

"What's in the back room?" asked Sam, somehow now intrigued by it.

Glenn clasped his hands tight together and pointed at Sam. "Well, it looks like you've already become just as much of a pain in the butt as these idiots," he said sarcastically. "You're already fittin' in perfectly," Glenn finished as he ignored Sam's question.

Silence filled the comic store as the wind gently brushed by.

It was so quiet that they could hear the beautiful birds singing in the bright green trees right outside of the comic shop.

It was so quiet you could hear the leaves rustling in the trees with each gust of wind.

It was so quiet that you could hear a butterfly's flapping wings as it looks for somewhere to rest.

It was so quiet that you could hear the steady breaths of each person in the comic shop.

It was so quiet...

Quiet...

Quiet..

Quiet.

"Soooo—" Johnny tapped the desk with his finger, "what's back there?"

Glenn looked back over at Johnny, surprised. "Honest-to-God I've got nothin' in that back room."

Johnny's face twisted up into several tiny nots and one eyebrow raised onto his forehead. "I'm not buyin' it."

"Here, listen—if you're really *that* curious as to what on Earth you think is in my backroom, just ask your friend!" Glenn pointed at Liam. "As far as I'm concerned, he's the only one here who has been in my backroom, and he'll tell you that there was absolutely nothin' back there worth seein'!"

"SO, THERE IS SOMETHIN' BACK THERE!" Johnny yelled out. "I KNEW IT!"

"What're you talkin' 'bout?" asked Glenn with a puzzled look.

"You said that there was nothin' *worth* seein'. Therefore, that means that there has to be somethin' back there!" Johnny crossed his arms with a smile stretched across his face as if he had just made a groundbreaking discovery.

"Of course, he has stuff back there, ya' idiot! Why else do you think he would have the room if he didn't use it for anything?" Jack asked, giving Johnny a slight nudge in the shoulder with his fist. "Honestly, how would you survive without us helpin' you out all the time!? I'm surprised you survived long enough to even meet us in the first place!" Jack shook his head in disappointment before returning his gaze right back on Glenn. "But, seriously," Jack slammed his hands down on the counter, "what's in the back room?"

"What part of you doesn't understand 'nothing'? Again, you can ask Liam if you'd like, but he'll tell you the same thing I did," Glenn said as he looked down at the three boys who continued to pester him.

"I don't buy it for a second!" Johnny said as he walked over to Liam and stared him straight into the eyes. "I have a hunch that you two made a deal."

Liam shook his head and began to chuckle to himself. "What're you talkin' about?"

"I believe that when you went back there you saw all kinds of treasures to behold," continued Johnny. "However, I don't know if Glenn threatened you or gave you money or what. All I know is that you know somethin' and for some reason you won't tell us."

Liam and Glenn shot each other a quick glance before bursting out into laughter. Glenn began to laugh so hard that he had to grab ahold of the counter for support as his legs began to give out. Liam grabbed ahold of Johnny's shoulders and continued to laugh. Everyone else just looked in confusion as Liam and Glenn continued to laugh.

"That's a good one, Johnny," Glenn said catching his breath and balance. He was still using the counter to support himself. "You almost had me there. Like, at first, I thought you were serious, but once I saw your face I understood."

"W-what are ya' talkin' about?" Johnny stammered. "I-I'm bein' serious. An' whatta'ya mean 'once you saw my face'? What the heck is wrong with my face!?"

"I-I dunno, but you shoulda seen it. It was hilarious!" Glenn began to burst out in laughter even more.

"Yeah, like the way it scrunched up in the front and your mouth curled nearly under your chin," Liam joined in.

"Oh, yeah, yeah! And the way your ears separated really far on either side of your face."

"An' both your eyebrows went up on your forehead but your eyes became even with your nostrils!"

"No, they definitely went below his nostrils!" Glenn corrected.

"You're probably right."

"Oh, but your hair. Somehow your hair stood up when you said it!" Glenn laughed.

"And his chin! Oh my God, his chin stuck out!"

"And his neck went back but his head and body went forward!"

"You were like a hunchback!" Liam continued to laugh.

Johnny nodded with a smirk across his face. "I see what you two are doin' here!" Johnny pointed at both of them. "You two are teasin' me."

"What're you talkin' about? We're just sayin' what we saw," Liam said.

"You guys are idiotic," Jack muttered under his breath.

"Yeah, just show us what's in the dang room!" Johnny yelled out. "Why on Earth would you be hidin' somethin' if it's not worth seein' in the first place!?"

"Come on—please!" Sam pleaded. "For a new-time customer?"

Glenn raised an eyebrow and his upper-lip curled. He took a deep breath in and then looked back at everyone. "Fine."

Everybody began to cheer.

"BUT!" Glenn pointed at the boys, "don't touch anythin'!"

"Okay!"

"Will do!"

"Yessir!"

Glenn walked over to the door and got out his keychain with three keys on it. He picked out one and began to unlock the door. The boys could hardly wait. They were jumping up and down and were treating this like the ending boss-fight in a video-game.

"I'm kinda nervous," Johnny leaned over and whispered to Jack.

"Same."

As the door of possibilities *creaked* open a gust of cool, refreshing air rushed over the boys. A bright, yellow light flowed out of the room and caused the whole store to glow gold.

"Whoa," Johnny put it simply as his jaw dangled beneath his head.

"You said it, brotha'," Jack replied. His face had the same look on it as Johnny's did and both of them refused to look away from the room.

"I don't get it?" Sam admitted as he blankly looked back and forth between dumbfounded Johnny and Jack.

Jack and Johnny continued to look through the door but refused to go through it. It was as if they were intimidated by the very act of stepping into a new place. They saw their dreams floating around in that room. They saw everything they imagined it would be: a full arcade packed into one single room, a movie theater—everything.

Sam saw a blank room with barren walls and a mattress on the floorboards. Just a few comic posters were hung up on the walls to hide the ugliness of the room.

"All these years of waiting—OF DREAMING— have finally come true. I have seen the unimaginable! I have seen the extraordinary! I have seen THE IMPOSSIBLE!" Johnny yelled in triumph as he raised his fist in the air in victory.

"It is everything I always hoped it would be..." Jack trailed off and began to tear up.

"I think their minds have wondered what's behind this door for so long that what they thought would be behind it is what they're seeing," Liam suggested.

Glenn looked down at Liam with fear. "Oh, no."

"What!?" Liam stammered.

"I have seen this before," Glenn paused.

"Well, get on with it!"

"They've gone mad with—"

"WITH WHAT!?"

"WITH MADNESS!" Glenn yelled out.

"Wow," Sam continued in the background, "everything about today has been very anti-climactic."

"Welcome to Kingston!" Glenn yelled.

"That should be our town slogan," Liam snickered.

"What? 'Welcome to Kingston'? I hate to break it to ya' but you're probably gonna have to come up with somethin' a bit better."

"No, not 'Welcome to Kingston'! It should be: 'Kingston, the Anti-Climactic'!"

Glenn paused and pondered for a second. "Ya' know what?"

"What?"

"That's not half bad."

"It is though," Sam said again in the background.

"Since when have you been so down beat?" asked Liam.

"I'm just screwin' with ya'!" Sam laughed. "What if we put up a sign when you entered the town that said that!?"

"How'd that work?" Liam asked.

"Well, we'd get a huge friggin' sign and we'd just put it right outside of Kingston," Sam stated.

"No, but how would we even get somethin' that big?"

"It doesn't matter," Glenn continued, "this is all just hypothetical. You're all just playin' 'what if?'."

Everyone paused as Sam and Liam looked at each other with grins on their faces.

"Oh, no! YOU CAN'T BE SERIOUS!" Glenn yelled.

"Oh, but, can't we?" asked Liam.

"I don't see why not," Sam stated.

"I see why not!" Glenn yelled.

"Okay, so we need paint and a sign and—" Sam trailed off.

"If you get caught you'll get fined!" Glenn stated.

"It's fine! You can just pay it off!" Liam said. "You own your own comic shop for cryin' out loud!"

"You heard Johnny! No customers! I HAVE NO CUSTOMERS!"

"We were just jokin'," Liam laughed.

"But it is kinda true," Sam murmured to himself.

"Listen, I can't just be there to bail you guys out if you get in trouble," Glenn said.

"Why not?" Sam asked.

"Well, because I-I," Glenn stuttered.

"You don't have a reason!" Liam concluded.

"I suspected as much," Sam shook his head.

"Have either of you taken time to think about how much trouble I could get into if you two actually go through with this?" Glenn asked.

"No."

"No, not really," Liam said plainly.

Everyone paused.

"Well?" Glenn asked.

"Well what? That was it," Liam said.

"Yeah. What're you talkin' about?" Sam asked.

"I take back what I said about likin' you," Glenn looked at Sam who started to chuckle.

"Yeah, he sort-of has a knack for doin' that," Liam laughed.

"Hey, don't you go ahead an' start talkin' now. I never said I liked you any more than I liked him," Glenn turned around and rested his head in his palms. "I'm too old for this," he murmured.

"You're seventeen," Liam stated.

"HE'S SEVENTEEN!?" Sam was surprised. "WITH THE WAY HE HAS BEEN ACTIN' I WAS THINKIN' AT LEAST THIRTY!"

"Yeah," Liam said, "not everyone that's young can actually be cool."

"I see what you two are tryin' to do here!" Glenn turned around and pointed at the two boys. "Do you really think that I care about bein' cool? I own a comic shop for cryin' out loud!"

"Yes."

"Yeah."

Glenn frowned as he looked down at the two boys. "Fine," he sighed, "meet me here tomorrow around noon. I will have already gotten the stuff ready and we can begin to head out."

"What!? Why tomorrow!?" Sam cried out.

"Hey! Do you want my help or not?" Glenn pointed at the boys.

"Yes," Sam frowned.

"Then we do this tomorrow around noon—like I said," Glenn closed his eyes and shook his head in disbelief as he walked away. "Can't believe I'm doing this."

After several minutes of standing in front of the backroom doorway Jack began to elbow Johnny.

"What is it?" Johnny whispered.

"Ya' think we should go in?" asked Jack.

"I'm kinda scared," Johnny shivered.

"Same time?" Jack asked.

Johnny nodded as he and Jack firmly grasped each other's hand and they slowly took a step through the doorway.

They both paused...

They both stopped...

They both let go of each other's hand...

"Wow," Jack continued, "there really is nothing in here."

"You said it, Jackio."

"Man, I can't believe that Glenn and Liam were telling the truth all along."

"I've waited this long to get into this room only to be disappointed," Johnny muttered.

"I know, right?"

"The most mysterious thing he has in here is a pile of sheets lying in the middle of the room."

"Why on Earth would he have a problem with us coming in here?" Jack asked.

"There's only one reasonable explanation," Johnny paused. "He is hiding something in here. We must search the place for anything worth seeing. Spread out!"

"Man," Liam continued, "I wish we could make the sign tonight. Johnny and Jack are probably gonna stay occupied with all these comics for a while so now would be the perfect time to do it."

"Yeah," Sam said, "the least we could do is collect the supplies tonight so it's ready by tomorrow. That seems reasonable."

Liam smiled as his eyes lit up. "HEY, HEY, HEY!"

"WHAT, WHAT, WHAT!?"

"Glenn said he wouldn't do the sign tonight but he never said that he wouldn't get the supplies for the sign tonight," Liam said as if he made a ground-breaking discovery.

"Well, we could always ask him."

"Yeah, and if he says 'no' then we could always just guilt trip him again like we just did earlier."

"Ehh, that wasn't really guilt tripping," Sam stated. "That was more like making him feel like a loser unless he did something with us."

"Isn't that what guilt tripping is?"

Sam shrugged, "I was always told that it was when you made somebody feel sorry for you. You made them feel like if they didn't do something for you that they were a bad person. That's guilt tripping."

"Give an example," Liam suggested.

"Okay, uhm," Sam paused, "like if a disabled guy wants to go somewhere so he asks you to take him there but then you're busy he could always just pull the 'I can never do anything myself because of these stupid legs' card."

"Ohhh, and then you would feel bad for not helping him," Liam nodded understandingly. "So, like, if it was a day after my birthday or my birthday was coming up I could just pull the 'Even though it's my birthday I never get what I want' card?"

"Exactly," Sam snapped his fingers.

"Okay, let's try it. It might work," Liam said.

Glenn turned around as he heard the two boys whispering amongst themselves. "Hey, what're you two talkin' about?"

Liam looked over at Sam and winked. "Well," Liam continued, "I was wondering if maybe we could go get the supplies tonight. Ya' know, that way you won't have to get them all by yourself tomorrow before we come back."

"Yeah, plus, I just moved here and don't have many fri—" Sam was cutoff.

"Sure. That's actually a great idea! I have nothing else better to do. The comic shop is about to close for the day anyway, and Johnny and Jack will probably stay occupied ransacking the backroom for a while."

Sam and Liam quickly looked at each other surprised by how easy it was to get Glenn to agree to their terms.

"Okay, so when do we go?" asked Liam.

"Well, how about now. Some of the stores are closing up so if we don't leave now we may have to do it another time," Glenn said as he pulled some car keys out of his pocket. "Okay Jack, and Johnny! Time to get out!"

Jack and Johnny walked out from the backroom in defeat. They hadn't found anything. Not a single thing of interest. Glenn closed the backroom door behind them and locked it. "Now, don't go in there. Just because there's nothing back there doesn't mean that I'm okay with you guys rummaging around my stuff and breaking everything I own. You guys can stay here and read comics. Me, Liam, and Sam are gonna go to the store for some reason." Glenn shook his head annoyingly. "I still have no idea why we're doing this."

Glenn walked toward the front door of the comic shop. As he opened it up the bell *dinged* and he flipped the **OPEN** sign around to say **CLOSED.** Liam and Sam stood there as they watched Glenn leave the comic shop without them. They waited for about thirty seconds staring blankly at the closed door before Glenn came back in and looked at the boys.

"Are you guys comin' or what?" he asked as he motioned for them to follow him.

Both of the boys immediately ran toward Glenn and out of the comic shop. Glenn locked the comic shop behind him.

"How're Johnny and Jack gonna get out?" asked Liam as Glenn proceeded to lock the front door to the shop.

Glenn shrugged. "They won't. Again, I have a feeling they're gonna be able to stay pretty pre-occupied with those comics of mine. I still have no idea why they think that I'm hiding something in the backroom. Liam, can you confirm... what is in that backroom?"

"Nothing."

"RIGHT YOU ARE!" Glenn yelled out. "There is absolutely nothing in that backroom, but they won't buy it."

"I kinda feel bad for them," Sam said. "They waited that long and nothing's back there."

"I don't," Glenn admitted. "They've been bugging me about that backroom for as long as I can remember. Liam included!"

Liam smirked.

Glenn took the keys out of the door. "I think the only reason that Liam wasn't so shocked that there was nothing in the room was because he was too occupied being shocked that Carol was in the comic shop at the same time he was."

Liam shook his head and rolled his eyes. "She's usually always in the comic shop when we are."

"Yeah, but you always get nervous around her," Glenn said.

"Tell me about it," Sam exclaimed.

"Wait, is there something I should know about? What're you talkin' about?" Glenn pointed to Sam.

"Well, apparently Liam let Carol borrow one of his comics."

"Continue," Glenn said.

"Well, she brought it back to him the next day in class. She said thanks and actually tried to start up a small convo with him—"

"Okay, I think that's enough for 'No-Show and All-Tell' today. Let's get goin'."

"Wait, I wanna see where this is going," Glenn admitted.

"The stores aren't gonna be open all night like you said! We need to get goin' now!" Liam continued as he looked around the parking lot. "Where's your car anyway?"

"We'll go right after the story," Glenn promised.

"Well, I'm gonna go look for the car," Liam said as he wondered around the store looking for Glenn's car.

Once Liam was gone Sam continued. "Well, like I was sayin' Carol was tryin' to talk to Liam. She said thanks and all that stuff for letting her borrow the comic in the first place. Liam couldn't take it. He started stuttering and all that crap."

"Are you serious!?" Glenn scoffed.

Sam nodded.

"WHERE THE HECK IS YOUR DANG CAR!?" Liam yelled from behind the back of the comic shop.

"COME AROUND FRONT AND WE'LL START HEADIN' THAT WAY!" Glenn yelled back.

Liam ran back around the comic shop until he was back at the front with Sam and Glenn.

"Where is it?" Liam asked.

"What, your pride? Oh, you left it at school when you couldn't hold up a normal conversation with Carol," Glenn teased.

"OHHH!" Sam laughed.

"Guys, come on. We don't have all night, like you guys said," Liam rolled his eyes.

"Come on, Liam," Sam said, "It's not even close to night." The sun was still almost in mid-sky even though it was already around 5:00 or 6:00 pm.

"Curse you long almost summer days!" Liam muttered. "It still doesn't change the time stores open and close, though."

"He's right," Glenn admitted, "we should get goin'. Just follow me and I'll show you where my car is," Glenn said as he started walking away from the comic shop.

Liam and Sam shrugged as they began to follow Glenn down the street.

"Where are we headed?" Liam asked once he and Sam caught up with Glenn.

Glenn paused for a second. "We're goin' to my dad's."

"Hmmm... there's somethin' in that backroom," Johnny stated as he stood in front of the locked door.

"What do you mean? You saw it for yourself. There's nothing in there."

"There has to be," Johnny said full of determination.

"No, there doesn't. And even if we did want to look around a bit more, how would we even get into the backroom? It's locked."

"I have my ways," Johnny rubbed his hands together, looking somewhat sinister.

"Just give up already."

"No!" Johnny stated, "I will never give up. Why else would he have locked us out of that room before they left. It's almost like he has something he doesn't want us to know about."

"Doubtfully," Jack responded.

"Well, I'm gonna find a way into that room, and I'm gonna prove everyone wrong!"

"Yeah, and while you do that I'll just be here reading comics," Jack replied as he pulled a comic off of the shelf, sat down on a bean-bag, and began to read as he flipped through the pages.

"So, you don't even want to see me try'n get into this room?"

"Considering I know you won't be able to get in it—no."

"What if I told you I could teach you how to pick a lock?" Johnny asked.

"As if! There is no way in the world that you know how to pick a lock," Jack stated.

"Oh, come on! I saw it in a movie once. I'm pretty sure I got this down."

"Well, if you get that door open, I'll help you look for something in that room," Jack promised.

Johnny smirked as he dug through his pockets for a bobby-pin. His pockets were always full of junk. Johnny quickly got down on his knees and jammed the bobby-pin in the lock of the door. He wiggled it as hard as he could, his face turning red with frustration, until finally he heard a click.

His eyes lit up.

Jack looked up from the bean-bag. "Holy crap," Jack ran over to Johnny as he threw the comics on the ground. "Did you actually do it?"

"Like I said—I saw it in a movie once," Johnny shrugged.

Jack shook his head in disbelief as they both walked into the backroom.

"This is it?" asked Sam in disbelief as he looked at the worn-down house that was falling all around itself.

"Yep, pretty awesome. I know," Glenn said sarcastically with a sad frown. "My dad, he lives here. He, uhm—" Glenn paused as he held back tears. "Technically this car is my dad's but he's always too drunk to notice it's gone, much less drive it in the first place." Glenn wiped under his eyes with his shirt sleeve. "I haven't seen him in a couple of months, despite working—or living, I should say—three minutes down the road from him. Shoot, as far as I know he's probably already drank himself to death. At the very least he's drank the memory of me out of his life plenty of times over again."

Liam and Sam didn't say anything. They didn't need to. Liam just rested a hand on Glenn's shoulder as they all stood there in the driveway.

"My mom, I don't know who she is. As far as I know he killed her when he came home too drunk to know what he was doing one night. He won't talk about her. He claims he doesn't remember her. He claims she just packed up her bags and left one day." Glenn sniffled, "Hell, I don't blame her. If I were her I would've left too. The only difference is that I would've left long before she did."

The yellow crisp grass rustled behind them as the wind blew from the East as if it, too, was trying to escape. The wind was running away just like Glenn had always wanted to. It didn't care where it was going. Just far away from there. Far away from that *place*. It was heading towards the sun. Half of it just wanted to leave and the other half hoped that they would actually run into the sun. Either way it would be a new start. Either way they would be somewhere better than where they left off.

Glenn's eyes glistened as the sun got closer and closer to the ground with each passing minute. And with each passing minute the sky began to turn different colors. Different colors of orange and pink and blue. Different colors of the soon-to-be night sky. Different colors of the world.

Everyone's hair swayed to their right as they remained silent in front of the house. It was almost as if the wind was tugging at their hair and clothes. Warning them. Telling them to leave before it was too late. Trying to save them.

Glenn recognized this feeling. It was the same feeling that swelled up inside his stomach when he was a kid and his dad had too much to drink. It was every punch in the gut he had received whenever he accidently misspoke. It was every slap across the face whenever he didn't respond. It was every black eye that popped up whenever he brought up his mom. It was every scar that he would have to hide for the rest of his life because his dad was too foolish to see that he was in the wrong. It was every scar that he would have to hide because his dad was angered easily. It was every scar that he would have to hide because his dad drank too much. It was every scar that he would have to hide because he wasn't strong enough. It was every scar he would have to hide because his mom left. His mom left him with that *monster*. His mom left him alone. His mom left him without help. His mom should've taken him with her but she didn't. His mom just left.

"Come on, guys," Glenn finally broke the silence as he jingled his keys around in his hand. "Let's get goin'. Like you said, Liam, we don't have all night. The stores'll be closing soon." Glenn walked into the open garage with a Cadillac Cimarron waiting for them inside. He opened the front door and hopped in the driver's seat. Liam hopped in next to Glenn in the passenger seat and Sam got in the back.

"LET'S GET THIS BABY ROLLIN'!" Glenn yelled out with a sudden burst of enthusiasm. He quickly started up the car and kicked it into reverse as he backed out of the driveway and onto the road.

"This is kinda like looking for buried..." Jack paused, "treasure?"

"More like buried secrets," Johnny said as he stood in the middle of the—for the most part—empty room.

"Okay," Jack continued, "let's start looking for some more *buried secrets*."

Johnny nodded as Jack and he began to ransack the room

"So," Glenn continued, "why'd you move here, Sam? Family?"

"No, uhm, actually it's something else."

"Well, feel free to tell me if you want, but I understand if it's personal," Glenn said.

"No, it's fine. I actually haven't told anyone why I moved here yet. It might feel good to finally get some stuff off of my chest."

"Okay, so let's hear it," Glenn suggested.

"Well, I don't know if you knew this but I have autism. I think Liam and Jack and Johnny already knew but most people don't."

"Yeah, well, I couldn't tell. You seem normal to me. Well, normal compared to Liam, Jack and Johnny but that doesn't really count for much."

"HEY!" Liam shot.

Sam chuckled, "I know, right?"

Glenn began to chuckle as well.

"So, yeah, as I was sayin'—" Sam paused and took a minute to gather his thoughts, "—I actually moved here from Michigan."

"Wow! Long ways from home, huh?"

"Tell me about it."

"I bet it's pretty hard to get used to these hot summers—or beginning of summers—down here."

"Yeah," Sam gasped.

"What's it like in Michigan?" Glenn asked.

"I dunno," Sam shrugged, "just like here, I guess. Just colder."

Glenn nodded. "Oh, I'm sorry, I got off track. Why'd you move here? And again, if it's personal I completely understand."

"Well, something happened at my school—"

"Mhm."

"—and I had one of my panic attacks again. Long story short, I had to move because the school I was going to wasn't working out and the doctors suggested that I find a different school to go to."

"Do you mind me asking what caused the panic attack?" Glenn asked.

"These kids—I don't know them—they just ran up to me one day and shoved me in one of their lockers. I was stuck in there for a couple of minutes before I started hyperventilating and the rest of that day is mainly a blur."

"How long were you stuck in the locker—do you know?" Glenn asked.

"Everyone told me that I was in there for a couple hours. My mom even came close to filing a 'Missing Person' report because I wasn't there when she came to pick me up that day."

"I'm sorry."

"The doctors said that the reason I couldn't remember anything was because when they found me I was passed out. They said that I was breathing too fast in such a tight space that I ran out of air."

"Was that your first panic attack?"

"Oh, no. I've had a lot, but the older I get the worse they get. That's why the doctors suggested that I go to a different school."

"So, why'd you pick Kingston?"

"Actually, I guess it is kinda family. My grandpa lives around here but I don't see him often. He's getting really old. Also, we just thought that a small school would do me some good."

Everyone got silent.

"I'm sorry," Glenn finally said. "That blows."

"The doctors said that if I have another panic attack, judging by the way things have been progressing so far, that I should move again."

"Wow, I had no idea," Liam continued. "Why didn't you tell me?"

"I just did."

"I mean sooner?"

Sam shrugged. "I guess the time just never seemed right, ya' know?"

Liam nodded. "Yeah, I get it."

Silence filled the car.

"So, who wants to listen to the radio?" Glenn asked.

"Sure."

"Sounds good."

Glenn turned the knobs on the radio to '102.7' or 'KJ 103' as a relatively new song began to play and everyone began to sing along.

> *"You put the boom-boom into my heart!*
> *You send my soul sky high when your lovin' starts!*
> *A jitterbug into my brain!*
> *It goes a bang-bang-bang till my feet do the same!*
> *But something's buggin' you,*
> *Something ain't right,*
> *My best friend told me what you did last night!*
> *You left me sleepin' in my bed!*
> *I was dreamin' but I should've been with you instead!*
> *Wake me up before you go-go!*
> *Don't leave me hangin' on like a yo-yo!*
> *Wake me up before you go-go!*
> *I don't want to miss it when you hit that high!*
> *So, wake me up before you go-go!"*

And as they continued to sing they drove down the road together.

"I'm starting to be convinced that there really *is* nothing in here," Jack said as he sat in the middle of the torn-apart room.

"Oh, come on, Jackio!" Johnny said as he sat down next to him on the floor. "We've got nothin' better to do. We're locked in this comic shop for God knows how long until Glenn gets back so we might as well keep searching."

"Well, we've searched this whole area and unless there's another room we haven't searched then I'd say it's a lost cause."

"So, what if there is a secret room?" Johnny asked.

"There's not a secret room."

"But what if?"

"Well," Jack squinted, "hypothetically—"

"Yes, hypothetically of course..."

"Hypothetically, if there was a secret room we probably would've found it by now. Also, we've been goin' to this comic shop for a long time so at the very least we would've known about it by now."

"I dunno. Glenn seems to be very good about keeping buried secrets a secret."

"Or he just may not have any secrets."

"Buried secrets," Johnny corrected.

"Fine! Buried secrets. Why are you even calling it that?"

"I dunno. Sounds kinda ominous, don't ya' think?" Johnny asked.

"Ominous?" Jack asked surprised, "do you even know what that word means?"

Johnny paused, "Well, no—but that's beside the point."

"Something's wrong with you."

"Whatever, man!" Johnny stood up and continued to search around the room. "I'm gonna keep lookin'."

"So, on the topic of admitting things or telling each other very emotional stuff that we've never told anyone before—who would like to be the next one to talk?" Glenn asked as he turned off the radio.

The car got quiet.

"Well, the way I see it is that you've already talked about your dad, I've already talked about why I had to move, so it'd only be fair if Liam told us emotional crap," Sam pointed out.

"Yeah! Ya' know what, Sam—GREAT IDEA! Let's hear it, Liam!" Glenn said.

"Well, uhm, I don't really have anything emotional that I really have to get off of my chest at the moment."

"Oh, come on! There's not anything that's been building up over a while?" Glenn asked.

"Not that I can think of."

"Nothin' at school that's botherin' ya'?"

"Not since about a week ago," Liam said, "but I already told you, Glenn."

"What? What happened about a week ago?" Sam asked.

"Oh, right! Sorry, I forgot that you hadn't moved here yet. It doesn't really feel like you're new here. It actually kinda feels like you've been livin' here for a while."

"Stop stalling!" Sam commanded, "Just tell me. I won't judge."

"Well, there is this group of kids that have been picking on us for a long while now. Last week they met us at the comic shop with a bunch of guys and were probably hoping to just beat the crap out of us. We, uhm, rode our bikes into the woods and hid out there for a while but they still found us."

"Did they beat you up?" asked Sam.

"No," Liam chuckled, "they didn't beat us up. They just got the new comic we bought and tore it to shreds. I think they would've probably pounded Jack's face in if Ricky hadn't told them to lay off."

"Well, what happened afterwards?"

"Well, I went back to the comic shop and was crying a bit."

"Crying!? Why were you crying?"

"Well, I wasn't upset about them tearing the comic up really, and I wasn't too scared of them—it was just the principle of the whole matter. The fact that they thought they ruled over us or somethin'. They thought they could do anything they wanted without having to pay the price because we were just nobodies and they were kings.

"Again, I wasn't upset about the comic book or even scared for that matter. I was just angry. I-I was furious that they thought they were so much better and stronger than us that they could just knock us around whenever they wanted."

Everyone paused.

Even though it was getting pretty late the sun was still looming above them as it turned the sky pink. The trees swayed in the summer wind as the long, yellow, uncut grass blew in the same direction. Liam stared out of his window and was happy that he had gotten that off of his chest. Glenn and Sam were right. He did have something that was balling up inside of him that he needed to let go. Everyone did. And as Liam continued to stare out his window he saw his own reflection and he smiled.

"HEY, JACKIO! LOOK AT THIS!" Johnny yelled as Jack continued to lay on the floor in the middle of the room.

"What, did you find somethin'?"

"YEAH! COME HERE!" Johnny quickly signaled for Jack to hurry.

Jack rolled his eyes as he stood up and walked over to Johnny. "What did you find?"

"Just look," Johnny said as his eyes lit up. He slowly pulled a book out of a bookcase in the room. It was the only type of decoration or furniture in there. Jack waited anxiously expecting the bookcase to sink into the ground only to reveal a hidden room.

It didn't.

"What is it?" Jack snarked.

"What? Don't you see it?" Johnny asked as he peered into the hole of the bookcase where he just pulled the book out of. "There's a handle, which means that there's a door."

Jack's frown immediately turned into a mischievous grin that stretched across his face. "Which means that there's another room in here— which also means that there are buried secrets!"

"RIGHT-IO JACKIO!" Johnny yelled out as he hopped up into the air anxiously.

Jack didn't care what Johnny had just called him, he just continued to grin. He couldn't for the life of him make it go away. "Okay, okay, okay—so w-what now?" Jack questioned as Johnny continued to do his embarrassing victory dance.

Johnny stopped and grabbed Jack by the shoulders. He pulled Jack closer to him and then quietly said, "We push the bookcase aside and see what type of secrets are in there." Even though there was nobody else around them Johnny still felt the need to whisper it. He was afraid that someone might steal his buried secrets.

"Okay," Jack stammered, "we push the bookcase aside—we walk through the door—we see what's through there—and then what?"

"And then what?" Johnny mocked, "We put everything back the way we found it OF COURSE! If Glenn really does have some stuff hidden away in here then we need to make sure that he doesn't know that we know that he has some secret stuff buried in this secret room."

"Right," Jack agreed and then he paused, "but why?"

Johnny took a deep breath in and slowly shook his head in disappointment. "Jackio, Jackio, Jackio—when will you ever learn? Have you ever heard of blackmail?"

"Yeah, but why would we need to blackmail Glenn?" Jack asked.

"I dunno! It's undecided. Maybe if there's somethin' we want in the future we could use whatever is in that room against him."

"Like if we want a free comic?"

"Think bigger," Johnny demanded.

"A free meal?"

"Bigger-er!"

"A CAR!?"

"Okay, well, don't get ahead of yourself, Jackio. We're not tryin' to make Glenn go bankrupt here. We're just tryin' to use good ol' fair blackmail to get stuff we want."

"Fair and square."

"Fair and square," Johnny confirmed.

"Well, here we are," Glenn said as he parked his car in the empty parking lot in front of Walmart.

"Hey, why did you say that we better hurry before it closed? I thought Walmart was open 24/7," Sam said.

"Liam was the one that said we should hurry. I just agreed with him," Glenn admitted.

"Well, I thought we were gonna go to that Paint N' Supplies shop back there," Liam admitted as he jabbed a thumb over his shoulder behind them.

"I mean, that's where I thought we were goin' too but then I saw that they had a closed sign up so I just came here instead."

"Okay, so what's the plan?" Sam asked as he stepped out of the car.

"Well, I say we should each grab a cart and grab as many supplies as we can. One person can be in charge of the sign and the other person can be in charge of the paint," Glenn said.

"What about the third person?" Sam asked.

"I dunno. I guess I'll just get extra supplies we may want to decorate it with."

"Nah, we don't need that," Liam said, "just help me get some paint. If the sign is really gonna be as big as I think it is then we're gonna need a lot of it. We'll each get a cart and we'll each get one of every color so in the end we'll have doubled up on everything."

"What about the poles to hold up the sign?" Sam asked, "And how big were you thinkin'?"

Liam shrugged, "I guess Glenn can just get the poles. Nevermind about the doubling up on paint. I can just get it all myself."

"And the size of the sign?"

Liam shrugged. "Just get the biggest one that you can find."

Sam nodded.

"OKAY!" Glenn clapped his hands. "I HAVE POLES, SAM HAS THE SIGN, AND LIAM HAS PAINT! LET'S GET GOING!"

And with that said, they all took off into the store.

Johnny and Jack strained as they tried to push the huge bookcase aside that was blocking the secret door.

"Shoot!" Jack yelled out as he collapsed to the floor in a sweat.

"Come on, Jackio! We haven't even been pushin' it that long," Johnny said as he reached down to give Jack a hand. "We can do it, and when we do we'll find what we've been looking for all along." Johnny quickly pulled out his inhaler, used it, and then put it back into his pocket. His right hand remained down to help Jack up. "Come on," he said.

Jack smirked as he reached up and grabbed his hand.

"So, now that we have everything where are we gonna keep your car?" asked Liam.

"Well, I suppose we're just gonna put it back in my dad's garage. He won't notice," Glenn reassured.

Sam nodded, "Okay. And then we'll just go back to the comic shop."

"Yep," Liam stated.

"I already have 'nuff goin' on tomorrow helpin' you two set up this god-forsaken sign," Glenn shook his head.

"The sign of Kingston!" sighed Liam as he leaned back in the car seat. "Tomorrow's bound to be exciting!"

"You guys better not get me caught by helpin' you set up this sign tomorrow," Glenn said as he pulled the car into the driveway of his old, torn down house that was already falling apart. Glenn turned the ignition off and stuck the keys in his pocket. He quietly got out of his car and motioned for Liam and Sam to do the same as he tiptoed down the street towards the comic shop.

"So," Glenn began once they were far enough away from the house, "*Kingston the Anti-Climactic*—is that really what you're gonna put on the sign?"

Liam shrugged, "Unless we think of somethin' else that would be better before tomorrow."

"Are Johnny and Jack comin'?" Glenn asked.

"Nah," Liam continued, "Johnny's dad is takin' him hunting for a racoon tomorrow and Jack is too paranoid to do somethin' like this."

"So, don't tell Jack?" Glenn asked.

"Don't tell Jack," Sam and Liam confirmed at the same time.

"Okay," Glenn nodded, "it's our secret until we're caught and I'm forced to pay a fine."

"We're not gettin' caught," Liam said, "it'll be fun. They don't really have many un-fun cops around here anyway. If they see what we're doin' they'll probably just laugh and tell us to take it down. A verbal warning at most."

"And how do you know all this?" Sam asked.

"I know a lot of people in this town. Everyone knows everyone here. The cops are usually parents to some kids that I know at my school," Liam stated.

"He's not wrong," Glenn continued, "about the 'everyone knows everyone' part. It is a small town."

"Yeah, you'll probably know most of the town by the end of Summer break."

D

I

N

G!

The bell that sat on top of the door *jingled* as they all walked into the store.

"JOHNNY!? JACK!?" Liam called out once they were in the store.

"IN HERE!" Johnny's voice came from the back room.

Everyone walked into the back room only to see Jack and Johnny trying to push aside a huge bookcase.

"What're you guys doin'?" Glenn asked as he walked over to them. "I told you guys not to come in here. How did you get in here?"

"No, there's something' behi—" Jack was cutoff.

"I think that it's time for everyone to go home," Glenn continued, "It's getting very late."

"No, but there really is someth—" Johnny was cutoff.

"Okay, okay, okay," Glenn said as he pushed Jack and Johnny out of the back room. "I know you probably didn't find what you were lookin' for, but that's okay. I did tell you not to go in the backroom, didn't I?"

"There's somethin' behind the boo—"

"Okay," Glenn smiled, "you all head on home. I'm gonna get this room cleaned up." Glenn closed the door with all the boys standing outside in the main lobby of the comic shop with a *SLAM!*

Johnny and Jack immediately turned to Liam and whispered, "There was somethin' behind that bookcase."

Liam just rolled his eyes and shook his head.

"We're bein' serious!" Jack said.

"Yeah, we swear!" Johnny crossed his heart with his finger.

"Okay, sure—whatever," Liam rolled his eyes again.

Sam looked up at Jack and Johnny with annoyance in his eyes.

"OH MY GOD!" Johnny yelled as he and Jack stomped out of the comic shop and hopped onto their bicycles angrily and began to pedal.

Sam and Liam began to laugh.

"You think there really is somethin' behind the bookcase?" Sam asked.

Liam shook his head. "No, but even if there is it's Glenn's and if he doesn't want to share it with us yet that's fine."

Sam nodded, "Yeah." He slowly looked around the comic shop, "I better get goin' home."

"Yeah," Liam said, "I'll see ya' tomorrow."

"See ya'," Sam said as he walked out of the comic shop and hopped on his bicycle and began to pedal home.

Liam smiled as he looked outside. It was still fairly bright. He slowly walked out of the comic shop. "Hey, Gabe," Liam said as he looked down at Gabe.

Gabe had a brown dress hat protecting his face from the sun as he sat against the comic shop's red, cracked brick wall. At the sound of Liam's voice Gabe jolted a bit and then slowly reached for the brown hat covering his face with his calloused, wrinkled old hands. He slowly lifted the hat off of his face allowing a beam of sun to burn his face with an orange warmth he hadn't felt since he put it on. His one blind eye and one warm brown eye peaked from underneath the hat and up at Liam who was standing in front of him. Gabe smiled. He didn't need to say anything. He just patted the hot concrete in front of the comic shop next to him with his hand.

"It's getting' hot isn't it?" Liam asked as he took a seat next to Gabe. "I'm surprised you haven't burnt yet." And as Liam took a seat on the hot concrete, not only did it burn him, but it sent a chill up his spine. The concrete not only felt hot but cold to the touch. A cold touch that was unfamiliar. Perhaps that was why it was so cold. It was different. It was new to him.

"Well," Gabe's raspy voice came from underneath the brown hat that Liam had given him so long ago," if it weren't for this ol' hat I prob'ly would be." Gabe smirked. And with the smirk came a glimmer. A glimmer of recognition. He remembered. Yes, he remembered. A face that for so long had a shadow cast over it he almost forgot what exactly it looked like. The smirk brought it back. Of all things it was the smirk. The smirk reminded Liam of his uncle. His kind, loving, father-like uncle. Liam smiled and stared off into the distance.

A gust a refreshing air swept by, almost taking Gabe's hat with it. Thankfully he had a hand on top of it and the wind was no match for him. The myrtle trees swayed in the distance as blooms of white and purple signaled the beginning of summer. And with every new gust of wind a different petal would get carried off of the tree and into the unknown. Who knew where the wind was taking it. It was gone though. It was alone. Starting its' own journey away from their friends and family. Perhaps it would travel the world or find a new home. Perhaps it would settle somewhere new and make new friends. Maybe it was just leaving for a while only to return a little while later. No one knew. Nobody could know. Perhaps the petal itself didn't even know. Maybe that little white petal that was carried away by the wind just knew that it needed something different. So, instead of staying in the comfort of the trees and with its' family it let go. It detached itself from the blossoming limbs of its' home branch. It was not only a sign of summer. It was a sign of change. A sign of something new. A sign of growing up. A sign of leaving everyone that you love to pursue your passion. A sign of change. Yes, a sign of change.

The pink sun set in front of Gabe and Liam as they sat against the cold brick wall, the rumbling of train tracks in the distance echoing through the streets. A shadow was cast off the myrtle tree back onto the brick wall and you could watch as the individual petals traveled just as fluidly in the shadow as they did in person. And as the blossoms were carried off into the wind, one pink blossom made its way over to Gabe. He held out his hand as the small pink petal landed ever-so-gently in the middle of his palm. Gabe looked over at Liam and handed him the pink petal with a gentle touch. Liam swept it in one of his hands and gently blew it away to let the wind take hold of it and carry it somewhere else.

Somewhere far away...

End of "Tracks" Book One...